An Offer for a Spinster

Willoughby #1

HISTORICAL REGENCY ROMANCE NOVEL

Katharine Willoughby
Timothy Rutherford

Dorothy Sheldon

Copyright © 2024 by Dorothy Sheldon
All Rights Reserved.
This book may not be reproduced or transmitted in any form without the written permission of the publisher. In no way is it legal to reproduce, duplicate, or transmit any part of this document in either electronic means or in printed format. Recording of this publication is strictly prohibited and any storage of this document is not allowed unless with written permission from the publisher.

Table of Contents

Prologue 4
Chapter One 13
Chapter Two 20
Chapter Three 26
Chapter Four 35
Chapter Five 44
Chapter Six 53
Chapter Seven 62
Chapter Eight 69
Chapter Nine 77
Chapter Ten 85
Chapter Eleven 93
Chapter Twelve 102
Chapter Thirteen 107
Chapter Fourteen 114
Chapter Fifteen 122
Chapter Sixteen 130
Chapter Seventeen 139
Chapter Eighteen 147
Chapter Nineteen 154

Chapter Twenty 161
Chapter Twenty-One 168
Chapter Twenty-Two... 175
Chapter Twenty-Three 179
Chapter Twenty-Four 183
Chapter Twenty-Five 187
Epilogue... 191

Prologue

Twelve Months Previously, the Dunleigh Estate

The door slammed hard, making Katherine flinch.

It was a fine day outside, sunshine streaming over the well-manicured grounds. Today was Saturday morning, and the Duke of Dunleigh always went riding on Saturday mornings.

Unfortunately for his children.

Katherine, pleading a headache, had shut herself up in the library. Her brothers would never have gotten away with such a trick, but the Duke didn't much care whether his daughter rode well or not. Ladies should, after all, confine themselves to carriages, in his opinion.

William, the oldest of the four, came storming in, disheveled and with a smear of mud on one cheek.

"I can't stand it a minute more, Kat," he gasped, breathless. "I can't *stand* it."

He was dressed for riding, the knees of his riding breeches muddied and torn, and was drawing in deep, shuddering breaths, like he might burst into tears at any moment.

Katherine closed her book with a snap, hurrying over to him.

"Oh, Will, I'm so sorry. Did that wretched horse try to kick you again?"

"Try? It succeeded. I know why he got that horse for me, Kat. He wants me to *master* it, but it's an impossible creature. I'm just so tired."

Katherine nibbled her lower lip, rubbing her brother's arm consolingly. She glanced out of the window, where she could now see figures moving around in a specially-build horse paddock out the front. There was the Duke himself, of course, tall, broad-shouldered, and no doubt grim-faced. The third Willoughby boy, the youngest of all four, was Alexander, hunched over in the corner of the paddock. It stood to reason that he would stay. Anything to secure their father's approval.

The second eldest of them all, Henry, was not here. He had gone on a Grand Tour, which was a great source of contention between the siblings. As a mere *woman*, Katherine would never have been permitted to go travelling. She doubted she would even be allowed to go on a local countryside walk without a handful of attendants. William had requested to go – just for a few months – and his request had been denied. He was, as the Duke had said, the eldest son, the heir, and had greater things on his mind than *travel*.

Henry's request, however, had been granted. The Duchess, who liked Henry the best out of them all, had been somewhat melancholy since he was gone. Apparently her other three children were a poor substitution.

Aside from the family, there was a knot of grooms, shifting nervously from foot to foot, eyeing the horse.

The horse in question was a fine creature, with a jet-black, glossy coat, a smooth black mane, massive hooves, and a well-arched neck. It was the largest horse Katherine had ever seen, as well as the most bad-tempered.

The horse was supposed to be William's new mount, which was all kinds of unfair.

"You must tell him you don't want to ride that horse." Kat said firmly. "It's going to break your neck if you keep trying. I don't think *anyone* can ride that bad-tempered creature."

William gave an angry snort, and shook his head. "Can you imagine what will happen if I do that? No, thank you, Kat. I don't care to be so thoroughly humiliated by my own father. It'll be his tale of choice at every dinner and party we throw, told round and round all the clubs and made more ridiculous until I'm described as a crying wretch in the corner." He broke off, throwing himself into a chair. "It's no use. He won't rest until I'm on that wretched horse."

Katherine sighed, turning back to the window. The Duke, her father, was standing to face the house now, fists on his hips, glowering up at her. He could surely see her in the window, and she automatically drew back.

The Willoughby siblings all resembled each other, famously so. They all had the same olive-tinged skin, the same hazel-green eyes – brown in some lights – and the same delicate chestnut locks. They were good-looking, all of them, and that always made things a little easier in Society.

The world loved pretty people, regardless of what was beneath the handsome exterior.

The Duke, for instance, was a remarkably handsome man, despite his age. And as such, there were people who still believed that he was a fair, generous, and good man, and a decent husband and father to boot.

"Listen, Will…" Katherine began, but was interrupted by the door creaking open.

Their mother stood there, and William dutifully bounced to his feet.

The poor Duchess of Dunleigh, Lady Mary Willoughby, was quite a faded woman. She'd been beautiful once, with rich blonde curls and a perfect porcelain skin, but time had not been kind to her. Even the light colour she'd had in her cheeks was long gone, and not one of her children resembled her. They all looked exactly like their father, much to their horror.

She folded her hands before her and looked severely at them both.

"Your Papa is summoning you, William," she said, in the light, tentative tones of a woman mostly used to staying silent. "He wants you to have another go at Midnight."

"If I try and ride that horse again, it'll break my neck," William said curtly. "Father knows it."

The Duchess shook her head. "Don't be so unkind. Your father only wants to improve your riding skills. You must go down, William."

Katherine watched the fight drain from her brother's face. He looked exhausted.

"Very well," he murmured, since they all knew that once the Duke had commanded something, it *had to* be done.

"I'll go with you," she said at once.

The Duchess frowned at her. "There's no need for that, Katherine. Why not practice your pianoforte instead? Your dear Papa said that you must practice more frequently."

Katherine loved hearing the pianoforte played but loathed playing it herself. She didn't let on, of course. Informing their beloved father of their distaste for any matter was a certain method of guaranteeing its frequent occurrence henceforth.

"I'd like to see the horse riding," Katherine said placidly.

The Duchess sighed in annoyance. "Very well, but bring your parasol. It's very sunny out there, and it will do your skin no good. You're already shockingly brown, Katherine."

The fashion was indeed for fair beauties at the moment, ladies with skin so pale one might assume that they'd never encountered even the concept of the sun. Katherine found it ridiculous, but one must pick one's battles.

So, she dutifully fetched her parasol, and scuttled after William and the Duchess onto the sun-drenched terrace.

William walked brusquely ahead of them all, head down, shoulders tight, and marched towards the horse paddock. The Duchess stayed on the terrace, where seats and tables were laid out, along with her embroidery, but Katherine followed her brother across the grass.

She heard her mother try and call her back, but the poor woman had never had a strong voice, and it was easy enough to ignore her.

"There you are," the Duke said shortly, glaring at William. "I don't expect any child of mine to give up so easily, William. Especially not the man who will be Duke of Dunleigh one day. I'm not entirely sure I *can* call you a man."

William lifted his head a little higher.

"I can't ride that wretched thing, Father. You know I can't."

"Are you afraid of a little tumble?"

"I'm afraid of breaking my neck."

The two men glared at each other for a long moment, and it occurred to Katherine – not for the first time – that the Duke and his eldest son resembled each other too well for anyone's comfort.

The Duke looked away first, his gaze sliding over William's shoulder to fix on Katherine, annoyed.

"Katherine, what are you doing out here?"

"I wanted to see the horse," Katherine said, as lightly and stupidly as she could manage. It was always easier to let her dear Papa see what he expected to see, which in her case was foolish but harmless good nature.

He snorted, shaking his head. "Very well. If nobody here is brave enough to climb onto a horse's back, I shall do it."

He turned his back, gesturing to one of the grooms. The man nervously hurried forward, snatching up the dangling reins of the big black horse.

A shiver of foreboding ran along Katherine's spine. William had his back to her, arms no doubt folded tightly, and was doubtless not in the mood to talk, so she edged along the fence to where Alexander stood. Her younger brother was stuffed into the corner of the paddock as if he were trying to squeeze through, arms folded tightly around himself.

"Is the horse really that bad tempered?" she whispered.

Alexander gave a short nod. "It kicked William when he was trying to mount it, even with all the grooms holding the creature still. It's half wild, Kat. I'm not sure anyone ever tried to break it in. It's a fine creature, certainly, but not easy to ride. I wouldn't dare ride it myself."

And yet the grooms were leading it over to the mounting block, and the Duke strode purposefully towards it. As Katherine watched, the horse snorted and bridled, huge hooves kicking up clouds of dust, scratching out grooves in the earth. She shuddered again.

"This is a bad idea," she murmured.

Alexander wet his lips nervously and stepped forward.

"Father," he said, his voice light and tremulous, "I'm not sure this is a good idea..."

That was a mistake, of course. The Duke cast him a quick, furious look, heavy with dislike, and did not deign to make a response. His look was enough, it seemed. Alexander shrunk back, visibly cowed, and wrapped his arms tighter around himself.

Katherine pressed her lips together and said nothing. All of them had gone through phases of trying to win their father's approval. For the most part, it was impossible, but Alexander had never quite given up. Lately, he seemed to think that conquests and gambling would impress the Duke.

They did not, naturally, but still, he persisted.

The horse reached the mounting block, and the Duke stepped up briskly. Before Katherine had time to suck in a breath, the Duke swung his leg over the horse's back, and settled himself in the saddle.

She breathed out, not daring to glance at William.

The grooms backed away, on edge, hands poised to catch the Duke should he fall. The horse snorted and pranced, ears going back, but the Duke kept his seat.

He allowed himself one tight smile, his cold blue gaze scanning his children.

"You see, William? All it takes is courage and confidence. I had flattered myself that you had both, to an extent. I was wrong, it seems."

Tapping his heels against the horse's flank, the Duke urged it forward. The horse's ears were still pinned back, and it jerked its head. The Duke kept a punishing grip on the reins, and Katherine saw blood and froth at the horse's mouth. She winced.

"Do you see, William?" the Duke called, a hint of triumph in his voice. The horse was walking forward, as quiet as a lamb, but she saw the tremor in the Duke's hands, and the way the reins strained.

"Papa, I..." Katherine began, not entirely sure what she intended to say or whether it would be listened to or not. "Papa, I really think..."

She never finished what she had to say. The horse jerked its head, yanking the reins out of the Duke's hand. It tossed its head, giving a horrible scream, and lurched forward.

Everybody cried out, running forward as if they could catch up to the creature. Clouds of dust and clods of earth kicked up behind the horse, raining down over them. She could see the Duke grabbing in vain for the reins, bouncing around in the saddle like a sack of potatoes.

But the paddock was not large, and the horse would surely have to turn... Katherine realised her mistake immediately. The horse was galloping towards the paddock fence and did not slow down.

"He's going to jump!" she heard a thin voice scream, a little shocked to discover it was her own. "He's going to jump the fence!"

Nobody responded. There was nothing anyone could do, and besides, they'd likely already worked that out.

The horse leapt, with a grace that Katherine had to admire even at a time like this, easily clearing the high fence, hooves leaving the ground.

Time seemed to slow, and she saw her father shifting in the saddle, trying in vain to adjust his balance, to weather a jump he had not been prepared for, still scrabbling at the reins in an attempt to retake control.

Perhaps that was his undoing, in the end.

Slowly, very slowly, it seemed, the Duke slid sideways out of the saddle. The seconds seemed to last forever. Strange flashes of memory impressed themselves in Katherine's mind – the sun glinting off the Duke's signet ring on his outstretched hand, one booted foot flying up to be silhouetted against the sun, a spray of grass falling around them.

Then the endless second passed, the horse hit the ground, and the Duke was underneath its hooves.

Thump.

Somebody screamed. The Duchess, perhaps, and commotion broke out.

The horse galloped away, kicking and rearing in an attempt to get the saddle off its back. The Duke lay still, in a crumpled heap on the ground.

The grooms raced forward, but William was quicker. He covered the length of the paddock in a blinking, vaulting the paddock fence as if it wasn't there, and dropped to his knees beside their father.

Katherine made to run after him, but Alexander grabbed her wrist, pulling her back. She'd dropped her parasol at some point, and the ridiculous lacy thing lay on the ground, a muddy smear of white.

"Alex, what are you doing?"

"You won't want to see," Alex said, his face bone white. "This isn't good, Katherine."

She pulled her wrist out of his grip and ran towards the Duke. The grooms were crowding around him now, and William was leaning over him.

She waited for the Duke to do something, to sit up, to groan, to start scolding someone – because it would never be his own fault that he'd fallen off a horse. He would have to blame the horse, naturally, or perhaps one of the grooms for not saddling it up properly. Perhaps he would blame William for distracting him, somehow.

But there was nothing. The Duke did not move, and he did not speak. The babble of voices got higher and more panicky, and a heavy weight of dread landed in Katherine's stomach.

Surely not.

William sat up, his hair wild and his face pale.

"Send for a doctor, at once!" he shouted to no one in particular. "It's an emergency!"

A handful of footmen scurried away, and Katherine watched them go. There was a pile of crumpled white fabric lying across the terrace, and it took her a moment to realize that it was their mother, having fainted.

She should probably go to her, but Katherine's feet felt as if they were rooted to the spot.

"William?" she called, hearing the tremor in her own voice. "William, is he badly hurt?"

Alexander appeared at her elbow, breathing raggedly and seeming on the brink of tears.

William sat back on his heels and met Katherine's eye squarely. She knew the truth then, before he had to say a word.

He said it anyway. Perhaps it didn't seem real, so saying it aloud made the truth of their situation sink in deeper.

Or perhaps William felt the same way as Katherine – the whole thing was surreal, almost funny, somewhat ridiculous.

"Somebody should write to Henry," Alexander said, under his breath, half to himself. "If we can get a letter to him, of course. He could be anywhere in the world right now, and I daresay he's lived in fear of a summons home."

Katherine shook her head, like a dog trying to get water out of its ears.

"William?" she asked again. William raked a hand through his hair. She noticed a splatter of blood on the white cuff of his sleeve, and she didn't think it was his own blood.

"He's dead, Katherine," William said bluntly. "Father is dead."

Chapter One

Present Day, London, Springtime

Holding her breath, Katherine turned a page in her novel. The fashionable etiquette handbook her mother had become addicted to since the funeral had a great deal to say about reading material in times of mourning.

Novels, needless to say, were heartily frowned upon.

Still, the Duchess – or Dowager Duchess, as she was now – was not quite as forceful as her husband had been, and only had heavy disapproval to threaten her children with.

It was quite freeing, not that Katherine would dare voice her opinions aloud.

To all intents and purposes, the Willoughby family was still in mourning after the tragic loss of their patriarch, the great Duke of Dunleigh himself. Consolations came rolling in, although notably, the second son of the family did not.

Henry, as Alexander had predicted, had been impossible to contact. Numerous letters were sent to him, explaining the situation and requesting his return home at once, since the will could not be read until his return.

No response had been forthcoming. In the end, just as the family was tentatively creeping out of mourning, a family friend had acted on a tip and gone to France, finding Henry in Paris, and bringing him disconsolately home.

Henry had never said whether he'd received the letters or not, and nobody had asked. It was easier that way.

He had naturally missed the funeral, of course, and was obliged to go into his own period of mourning since he'd missed the family mourning. They generally contented themselves with a black armband at this stage, and Henry was somewhat peeved to be plunged into deep mourning.

There was a sense of guilt among them all, that was generally not mentioned. For her part, Katherine had not been able to cry a single tear at the funeral, although thankfully her thick black veil had covered her face well enough.

There was a gentle tap on the door – that was something new, their mother knocking before she entered a room – and Katherine just had time to mark her place in the book before the Duchess sailed in, plucking the book from her hands and slamming it closed.

"Novels, Katherine?" the Duchess said, her voice dripping with displeasure. "You know how I feel about such things."

She eyed the title and shook her head. "*Rosalie's Trials, by L. Sterling.* This author is particularly crass."

"They are not *crass*. They're wonderful."

The Duchess snorted, tossing the book onto a nearby seat.

L. Sterling was a relatively new author, but their books were already sweeping the country. The critics, of course, decried them, preferring their books to have solid morals and heroines who did more Womanly things, like fainting and needing to be rescued.

Her current book, the second volume in Rosalie's adventures, was just as thrilling as all the others. Rosalie was a plucky and intelligent young woman, who was naturally enjoying a romance with a likeable young man, but also managed to do things by herself, and rescued herself quite frequently. It was a refreshing change, and the swooning was kept to a minimum.

"We're reading the will," the Duchess said shortly. "Meet us in the study at once, Katherine."

The Duchess turned on her heel and strode out, leaving a strong scent of rosewater in her wake.

Katherine didn't immediately follow. Since her father's death, it felt as if she'd lost two parents, instead of just one. The Duchess seemed to feel her husband's death more keenly than anyone else, although that made little sense to Katherine. The Duke had been just as cruel to his wife as he had been to his children.

Not the point, Katherine reminded herself. *He's dead. No need to be cruel. It doesn't matter what he did to us, or how he treated us. He died, and that's that.*

She rose to her feet, shaking out her skirts with a sigh. Part of her was excited, which only made the guilty feeling worse.

By the sounds of it, everyone was already gathered in the study already, the murmur of voices drifting out into the hall.

Katherine was the last to arrive. Seats were arranged in a semicircle in front of the late Duke's desk – she supposed that William was now the current Duke, although the estate had been in limbo while they waited for Henry to return – and the executor of the will, Mr Thompson, shifted from foot to foot behind the desk.

They all turned and looked at her, a trifle annoyed at the delay.

William's face was white and drawn – the last year had been troublesome for him. Henry was deeply tanned and looked rather too handsome and satisfied for a man who'd lost his father. Alexander looked miserable, his round face thinning out a little. Their mother, of course, seemed to have aged at least ten years.

Katherine knew that she looked more or less the same, if a little paler from all their time shut up in the house, mourning. She flashed a weak smile around and sat down beside Alexander.

A year ago, she would have preferred to sit beside William. It would be a lie to say she didn't have a favourite brother. But William had acted strangely since the accident, and of course Henry was distant as always. If he couldn't be *literally* distant from his family, he kept a neat emotional distance.

"Now that we are all here," Mr Thompson said, with the barest hint of reproach in his voice, "we can begin the will reading, which has long been delayed. His Grace the Duke of Dunleigh left a specific will. Naturally, the title and the entailed estate goes to his heir, Lord William Willoughby, but that leaves a vast part of the estate which must be divided. I shall begin."

Clearing his throat officiously, the man began to read. It started much as Katherine had expected, with a list of the late

Duke's belongings, wealth, estates, and so on. Some of it was connected to the title, so the new Duke of Dunleigh would inherit that, but what about the rest?

Katherine frowned, leaning forward in her seat. The executor appeared rather nervous. He was a thin, balding man, with wisps of grey hair at his ears, and too-tight pince-nez on his nose. He glanced frequently up at them, gaze flicking nervously around the room.

He must have already read the will, of course. What was he afraid of?

One by one, he listed the members of the family who would be provided for. The Duchess, being the primary heir, would naturally receive Dowager House along with a substantial jointure and a significant sum of money, easily enough to keep her in comfort for the rest of her life. He listed the sums of money each of his children would inherit. Only William inherited land and the estate, but Henry, Katherine, and Alexander would be tremendously wealthy in their own rights.

It had occurred to Katherine, of course, that their father would try some last-minute nastiness, like cutting somebody out of the will, or something equally spiteful. But no, he seemed to have provided for everybody. Katherine watched Alexander sink back into his seat with a relieved sigh and guessed that he had outstanding debts to pay off. She could almost see the maps revolving in Henry's head, thinking of where he would travel next.

As for herself, that money meant freedom. No need to marry, if she couldn't find a man who suited her. She could buy a house and live there by herself, if she liked.

I could travel, if I wanted. I can do what I like. I'm free.

The will seemed to come to an end, but Mr Thompson still stood there, eyeing them all nervously.

"His Grace added a stipulation to the will, shortly before his death," he said hesitantly. "He was concerned about what would become of his family after his death. I... I shall read what he wrote. 'In case my family should forget what is due of the Willoughbys and the great Dunleigh Estate, I have chosen to remind them. While I cannot stop my eldest son inheriting his title and the small amount of money attached to the estate, the rest of the property and money is mine to dispose of as I wish. The inheritance due to my widow will remain unchanged and unencumbered. However, before my children may access their inheritance, they are required to marry in a court of law. On the date of their marriage, they may receive their full inheritance, and…"

Clamor broke out. Henry leapt to his feet.

"We have to *marry*?" he shouted, clenching his fists. "All of us? Are you mad?"

Mr Thompson held out his hand in a placating gesture.

"Please, Lord Henry, let me finish…"

He was not allowed to finish. Alexander started to shout, and William was saying something, and the Duchess was crying, and Katherine found herself on her feet, trying to tug the will out of the poor lawyer's hands. He hung on grimly.

"This cannot be legal," William said, pitching his voice above the chaos.

Mr Thompson adjusted his pince-nez. "I am afraid that it is. You may try and break the will, if you like, but I can assure you it will take years, and the entire Dunleigh estate will likely be eaten up before it is settled. Regrettably, this will is completely impervious to challenge. If you wish to receive your inheritance, you must marry. You'll receive a small allowance each until that happens."

He named the sum, and Henry groaned aloud, sinking back into his seat. It *was* a paltry amount.

"So, all of us must marry to receive our inheritance, or can one of us marry and receive their money?" Alexander asked. Shockingly, he was the level-headed one today. The Duchess was still weeping quietly.

Mr Thompson fiddled with his pince-nez again.

"That brings me to my next point. Each may receive his inheritance once he marries, with one exception. Lady Katherine must marry first, before anyone can receive any money."

A heavy silence landed on the room. Katherine felt guilty over mocking those swooning heroines, as her knees buckled under her. Thankfully, a seat was there – Alexander to the rescue, she suspected – and she landed heavily in it, knocking the breath out of herself.

"So, if I don't marry," she heard herself say, voice wobbling, "nobody can get their inheritance?"

Silence. Everyone looked at Mr Thompson. The poor man – who really did not deserve this – drew in a breath.

"No," he said quietly. "They cannot."

Chaos again. William was arguing with Henry, Alexander was over at the desk trying to reason with Mr Thompson – as if that would do any good – and Katherine sat where she was, feeling as if she'd been turned to stone.

There'd be no money, then. No freedom for her. If she didn't marry, her entire family would be doomed to poverty. Henry and Alexander would be penniless, and William saddled with a title and estate he could not afford to run.

It all depended on her.

She recalled that fateful morning in the horse paddock, the way the Duke's gaze had slid over William's shoulder and landed on her, full of contempt and disapproval.

How he must have hated me, Katherine thought, tears pricking at her eyes. *Even dead, he wants to have the last laugh. He wants to control us.*

And he'd succeeded, quite nicely.

She considered getting to her feet. The study was too hot and stuffy, somehow, and she wanted so badly to get some fresh air, although her legs felt like jelly.

"There's more," Mr Thompson said, his voice wavering. Five pairs of eyes turned on him. No, four pairs, as the Duchess had fainted again.

"Tell us," William said heavily. "I'm not sure you can make it any worse."

Mr Thompson gave a nervous chuckle. "You have one year from the date of the reading of this will to secure a spouse and your inheritance. Whoever is not married will lose their money forever, and it will go to a distant relative. If Lady Katherine is not married, the entirety of the inheritance will be lost."

Katherine had worried about bursting into tears, but the reality was much worse. She started to laugh, high, hysterical giggles bubbling up out of her mouth no matter how hard she pressed her hand against it.

It's over, she thought dizzily. *It's all over.*

Chapter Two

The dedicated readers of L. Sterling might have been surprised to find their favourite author in such an unfashionable part of London, in an *apartment*, no less.

L. Sterling was, as the critics had speculated, a pseudonym. The author of *Rosalie's Trials* and various other books was a young man by the name of Timothy Rutherford, a mere second son, a simple *Mr.*

Timothy didn't much care what Society thought of his home. His income consisted of his money from the writing, and a small allowance from his mother's fortune. Not much, but enough to keep himself going. It allowed him to write, as he'd always wanted to, instead of clerking at some dreary law office or ingratiating himself with his father or older sibling. They'd make him jump through hoops for his money, and no mistake.

No, this method allowed him a little pride. He liked his apartment well enough and got on well with his landlady. Nobody knew he was L. Sterling, and even if someone put two and two together – Sterling was his mother's maiden name, and lilies were his favourite flower – well, it was a common enough name.

His little study was crammed with books, with a space cleared by the window just large enough to admit a small desk and chair. Crumpled bits of paper scattered across the floor, and a cold, half-drunk cup of tea stood forgotten on the edge of the desk.

The second volume of *Rosalie's Trials* was very well received, but he found that the third volume was coming along slowly. How to end the story in a satisfying way?

He sat back, crumpling up yet another piece of paper and tossing it onto the floor.

It's no good, he thought miserably. He took off his spectacles, wire-rimmed and round, and rubbed his sore eyes.

Timothy did not look much like the heroes he described in his books. Timothy himself was of average height, slimly built in a way a person might generously describe as *wiry*, with dark blond hair that would *not* go into the popular styles, and large green eyes.

As far as he could tell, his readers like strapping, classically handsome heroes, who did manly things like excessive horse riding and boxing. Timothy wryly flexed his own hands, white and elegant and decidedly *writer's* hands.

He didn't have time to sit and puzzle over Rosalie's next adventure, though. He had to get himself to the club to meet his friend. As far as he knew, the infamous Dunleigh will had finally been read, meaning that his friend William might now be excessively rich. How nice.

Shrugging himself into a somewhat patchy coat and clapping last season's hat on his head, Timothy firmly put Rosalie out of his mind, and headed out into the gray January day, collar turned up against the drizzling rain.

It will be good to know that somebody *has received good news recently. I bet the Willoughby family are celebrating as we speak.*

***

"That can't be right," Timothy said incredulously. "You must *all* marry?"

William looked exhausted. He'd drunk one large glass of brandy before Timothy had got there and was well into his second. There were dark bags under his eyes, and lines on his face that hadn't been there the last time Timothy saw him. They'd been friends for longer than he could remember, and William had had plenty to say about his father's cruelty.

This, however, was a new low.

"We can get some of it, if we don't *all* marry, but not all of it," William explained wearily. "But we can't get a penny unless Katherine marries. She must marry *first*. We've got a year."

"A year to find someone, or..."

"A year to *get* married."

Timothy blew out a heavy breath. That didn't leave a great deal of time. In London, the Season was just ramping up. That gave at least six months to find a person, as well as to organize the wedding and get the ceremony over with. For all of them. The Season was called the Marriage Mart for a reason, but to have a deadline like this was... well, it was something new.

"It's... it's doable, is it not?" Timothy heard himself say, somewhat lamely. No doubt they'd considered this, as well as all the angles.

William shrugged weakly. "I hadn't considered marriage. I have too many responsibilities, and I intended to spend a year or two as Duke of Dunleigh to acclimate myself before even thinking about marrying. I wanted to marry, of course, but to be forced into it..." he broke off, shaking his head. "Alexander hoped to marry an heiress, but on his own terms. Henry had never thought of marriage at all, as far as I know. And as for Katherine, do you know what she looked forward to most out of all this? Freedom. She longed for freedom. And now she'll never see a day of it."

A lump rose to Timothy's throat at the mention of Katherine.

He'd been friends with the Willoughby family for many years. *Friends*, of course, was a loose term.

Henry, the traveler, was somewhat aloof in London, preferring his friends abroad, and Alexander gambled too deeply and drank too much for Timothy's liking. Timothy and William were twenty-six, the same age, and had the most in common.

One thing they had in common was that the late Duke had not liked either of them.

Oh, and that Timothy knew exactly what it was like to have a father so deeply disappointed in you. He didn't want to bring that up now, of course. With the contents of the will, he assumed that William knew that already.

He'd only really known Katherine from a distance, but that was enough to discover that she was the most beautiful and interesting girl he'd never quite met.

Not helpful, Timothy told himself sternly. Aloud, he said, "Shall we go somewhere more private to talk?"

William shot him a quick grateful look. "Yes, I'd like that."

Their club of choice was White's, coincidentally the only one that Timothy was granted membership to. It was considered rather important that a man be *clubbable*, although he didn't much enjoy the process of attending clubs. His father and older brother would be mortified if he wasn't a member of at least one. Even Henry Willoughby, the man with his mind always elsewhere, was a member of White's.

The place was crowded, as it usually was at this time of day. It was all too easy for something to be overheard and repeated. Timothy led the way to a small alcove, just large enough for two men to sit on opposite armchairs, with a low coffee table in between. William drank down his own brandy in one large gulp, and snatched up another, following Timothy.

"I don't want this talked about," William muttered, settling down. "I know you'll be discreet, of course, but if this gets out... well, we'll be bombarded by hopeful mammas and fortune hunters. Alexander's a fool, Henry might well be stubborn enough to refuse to marry altogether, and as for me... well, I don't have much faith in my own judgement, to be frank."

Timothy leaned forward, propping up his elbows on his knees.

"That's your father talking, Will. Your judgement is fine."

William smiled bleakly. "Thank you, Timothy, that's kind of you to say. My father clearly thought that we'd all go unmarried and let the Willoughby name die out. Or else he just wanted to punish us. A bit of both, perhaps. I'm tired of trying to work out what he wanted, what he was thinking." He paused and gave a short laugh. "Even from beyond the grave, he's controlling us. It's impressive, when you think about it."

Impressive was not the word that sprang to mind, in Timothy's opinion. He pressed his lips together and shook his head.

"I hate to speak ill of the dead, but the man was evil. I'm sorry, William."

William shook his head. "Don't be. I'm worried most about Katherine. Out of all of us, she's the one who *must* marry, or else we'll all be paupers. I know exactly why Father set up the will in that way. We were all disappointments to him, but Katherine was the one he struggled most to break. I suppose he thought he'd manage it this way."

That lump rose to Timothy's throat again. He swallowed hard, trying to fight past the surge of anger he felt towards the man. How dared he ruin his children's life in this way? What was it all for?

The answer presented itself at once. The late Duke of Dunleigh believed that his children belonged to him, in the same way that his wife and house did, and it irked him that he could not control them the way he thought he could. The will was a final effort to do that.

Unless they all marry for love, Timothy thought. *Not that that's likely to happen.*

"Do you think Katherine will refuse to marry?" he heard himself say.

William shook his head. "No, not with all of our futures at stake. She's too kind. She may be careless with her own funds, but not with ours. It just means that her inheritance will never really be hers. It'll belong to her husband right away."

"Unless he agrees to let her keep it and signs a few legal documents."

William gave a hoarse laugh. "And who would agree to that? No, I'm afraid that if this gets out, she'll be surrounded by fortune hunters. Please, Timothy, you must join the Season this year, help me keep an eye on her. I can't trust Alexander to stay focused, or Henry. She's my only sister, and I do worry about her so much."

Timothy swallowed hard. His head was reeling, and his heart clenched worryingly.

Stop it, he scolded himself. *Be honorable. Protect your friend's sister, can't you? Put your own feelings aside – the woman scarcely knows you.*

He smiled weakly at William. "Of course, if that's what you want. I'll do my best. I can't promise to protect her properly, but…"

"No, no, that's fine. I'll feel better knowing that you're looking after her, too. As if she has a fourth brother."

"Yes," Timothy murmured bleakly. "A fourth brother."

"The thing is," William continued, rubbing his eyes, "she's twenty years old. This will be her third Season. She's hardly *old*, but you know how cruel Society can be. Even the doddery old men think they have a right to marry the eighteen-year-old debutantes. I'm worried that Katherine will simply marry the first man she meets. I'm afraid that she won't get many offers, and that she'll settle, for our sake. She's my sister, Timothy. I love her, and I can't bear the idea of her being unhappy. But I don't know what to *do*."

Timothy reached forward and laid a hand on his friend's shoulder. The good thing about being a writer was that words were always at one's disposal. Usually, at least.

When one had a piece of paper and pen to hand.

Now, though, it seemed that Timothy had hit a stroke of luck, and the words came easily.

"Katherine is stronger than you think," he said firmly. "She's clever, and thoughtful, and a good judge of people. Your siblings and you need to be closer now, more than ever before. You're all in the same boat, and your marriages will likely take place very close together. You're the head of the family now, William. You need to draw everyone together and present a united front. Your father spent his life pushing you all apart, but he never succeeded, did he? You can draw together now."

William swallowed hard, thinking it over. He nodded slowly, and Timothy felt a knot of anxiety loosen in his chest.

"You're right, Timothy. This is father's last attempt to control us, but if we take control of the situation first, we'll pull through." He swigged back his brandy in one gulp. "I'm glad we met up today."

Timothy smiled weakly, trying not to think about Katherine Willoughby walking down the aisle with a fortune hunter.

"Well, a problem shared is a problem halved."

I could marry her, he thought, and a strange tingling feeling rolled down his spine.

Chapter Three

"Is everything ready? Are we sure everything is ready?" Katherine asked, anxiously twisting around in her dressing-table chair.

Mrs. Ruth, the housekeeper, stood in the doorway to Katherine's bedroom, hands demurely folded, a neat smile on her face.

"Everything is ready, Lady Katherine." Mrs. Ruth assured her. "I have been taking care of these gatherings since before you were gone. Everything is perfect, I promise."

Katherine smiled faintly. The housekeeper and butler knew about the conditions of the will, but nobody else. It would never do for it to get out. The housekeeper, Mrs. Ruth, and the butler – incidentally Mr. Ruth, her husband – had served the family for decades, and would keep a secret faithfully.

"Now, if that's everything...?" Mrs. Ruth asked, and Katherine nodded, dismissing her.

Then there was nothing left to distract her from her own reflection and her own worries.

This evening was not the apex of the Season, not by any means, but somehow it felt more important than any of the other balls Katherine had intended.

She, and her brothers too, would have to go through tonight looking in earnest for a marriage mate. One year. One year really wasn't enough time, not to meet a new acquaintance, become sure of them, pursue an understanding, and then *marriage*! Oh, it scarcely bore thinking about.

Katherine closed her eyes, hoping to shut out her own image. Her maid, Sally, had put her in a deep mustard-coloured silk dress, simply cut but flattering, tightly bodiced and with a neckline that just skimmed the edge of daring. Her hair was done up, piled in loose curls on her head, the chestnut lights glimmering in the candlelight. Her skin was darker rather than lighter, but Katherine had long since given up wanting fair skin. Let the blonde ladies boast themselves as fair beauties if they liked.

The woman staring back at her seemed unfamiliar now, a mercenary lady on the hunt for a husband, at all costs.

If I don't marry, none of us will get a penny, she thought, for the thousandth time. *Everything rests on me.*

The thought had provoked a sharp pang of cold fear to start with, something icy and prickling, but now she was numb to it. It almost didn't feel real anymore, as if it were a line she'd read in a novel. A favourite novel, perhaps. An L. Sterling.

Don't think about books, or else you'll curl up on bed and read instead of going down to face your guests.

"There," Sally remarked, putting the last touches on Katherine's hair. "You look beautiful, milady, if I may say so."

"Thank you, Sally," Katherine said, flashing a tight smile. She'd have to do better than that throughout the evening. It would be nonstop smiling.

"Just in time," William remarked, as Katherine carefully descended the stairs. The ballroom, dining room, and surrounding hallways were all prepared for the ball, decorated with flowers and garlands – paper, silk, and real – and lit with countless candles. Like fairyland, hopefully. That, as far as she could tell from the gossip columns, was the highest praise a ball could get.

"Did you think I'd be late for our first ball after our mourning?" Katherine remarked. "You look very fine."

The four of them had chosen different colours, all designed to flatter their olive skin. A deep green for William, a burgundy for Alexander, and royal blue for Henry. It was, in Katherine's opinion, a good way to get noticed.

None of them had discussed much their plans for finding marriage mates.

It's alright for them, she thought sourly. *Their marriage need not change their lives at all.*

William offered an arm, gesturing for them to go through to the ballroom.

"Mr. and Mrs. Ruth have done a fabulous job. Nobody will be able to fault our decorations or food tonight, at the very least." He glanced pointedly over at Henry, who had thrown himself into a chair in the corner of the room, one leg thrown languidly over the arm. "I do hope you'll put that book away when our guests arrive, Henry."

"What of it?" Henry responded, not taking his eyes off the page. "So what if I don't?"

William pressed his lips together. "Don't, Henry."

"Don't what?"

"You know what. Not tonight. Society will be especially sharp with us."

Henry sighed, and pointedly turned a page.

"Leave him," Katherine murmured. "Henry always said that he wasn't sure if he'd like to marry at all. Having the choice taken away from him would certainly be smart. Henry enjoyed having control over his life.

Well, don't we all, Katherine thought bitterly. *And our dear father neatly took it all away from us.*

"I'm going to greet the guests as they come in," William said. "The three of you stay here to talk when people enter. Find Alexander, won't you, and take Henry's book away."

"I will."

Tonight wasn't going to be fun for anyone, then. William half turned away, then paused, and turned back.

"Oh, and my friend is coming tonight. Timothy Rutherford, do you remember him?"

Katherine blinked, and conjured up an image of a quiet, bespectacled young man she'd seen from a distance. "Vaguely, yes."

"He's arriving with his aunt. Do make him welcome, won't you? He doesn't much enjoy balls."

"I'll do my best. No promises, though."

William shot her a tight, brave smile, and departed.

So it begins, she thought, feeling the odd, giddy desire to laugh again.

The ball began and rolled on with very little help from the Willoughby siblings. Katherine caught glimpses of her brothers here and there – a flash of Alexander's burgundy coat as he chatted to a group of chaperones and their youthful quarries, or Henry bringing drinks for some young lady and gentleman. William was everywhere, the perfect host, and the ideal new duke.

Katherine was proud of him, frankly.

For herself, a ball like this was all duty. People who had to be greeted, pleasantries that had to be exchanged, and so forth. Her dance card was quickly filled, with only a few spaces remaining, and her feet were already aching. She'd received countless compliments on her looks, although some compliments were laced with disapproval – as if it were disloyal to look so pretty after the death of one's father. The dowager Duchess, after all, was still in black.

Katherine mostly tried to avoid her mother's eye. The Duchess sat in the corner, draped in black silk and pearls like a woman twenty years older.

"I know it's not at all the thing to speak to a person without being introduced," came a low, male voice in her ear, "but I've been trying to get introduced to Lady Katherine Willoughby all night, and no luck."

Flinching, Katherine turned to see who was speaking to her.

A tall, handsome gentleman stood there, with broad shoulders and a broad smile. He had a mop of rich black curls, and wore a new suit in the latest fashion, an unusual shade of burnt orange.

"I… I believe you have the advantage of me," Katherine managed. He wasn't looming over her, at least.

"Of course, do forgive me. I could fetch the Duchess, if you like, to make a proper introduction."

"No, no, that won't be necessary. I won't tell if you don't."

He smiled at that. "My name is Lord Geoffrey Barrington, Earl of Barwood. I've spent most of my life in the Americas, I've only been back these past few months. I was a business acquaintance of your late father's. Please, accept my condolences."

The name seemed vaguely familiar. Had the Duke mentioned him before? Most likely.

"It's a great pleasure," Katherine responded, dropping a neat curtsey.

She wasn't entirely sure it would be anything of the sort. A friend of her father's was not likely to be a particularly *pleasant* man.

Not that Lord Barwood seemed unpleasant. He talked lightly, exchanging the usual comments and remarks a person made at balls, where it was too loud to hear one's partner properly.

"I take it you are dancing, Lady Katherine?" he queried, after a moment or two of this.

"Of course. I am opening the ball with my brother, William."

"Could I be so bold as to request a dance?"

Katherine hesitated, checking her dance card. "I have some spaces, yes."

"How wonderful. I've heard that you are a talented dancer."

She chuckled. "Every woman here can list *dancing* as an accomplishment."

"I think you can also add an impressive list of admirers to your accomplishments, too," Lord Barwood added, gaze sliding over her shoulder. "That gentleman over there is staring at you."

She glanced behind her and saw immediately who Lord Barwood meant.

A wiry-looking young man with disheveled blond curls and green eyes behind circular spectacles was hovering at a distance. He flushed when he realized he'd been spotted and came edging forward.

"Do forgive me, Lady Katherine," he murmured. "Only, William asked me to come and check on you, as he's scarcely caught a glimpse of you all night."

"Ah," Katherine said, with dawning understanding. "Lord Barwood, this is Mr. Timothy Rutherford. He's an old friend of my brother's. I haven't seen you in a long time, Mr. Rutherford."

"Yes, it has been a while," Timothy said, laughing nervously. "William was concerned you might be getting tired, only he couldn't get away from Lord and Lady Edrington, and…"

"I'm quite alright, thank you. I'm gathering my strength for the dancing, which begins soon."

Timothy nodded. He glanced briefly at Lord Barwood, who was inspecting him with a long, blank stare. Not a particularly welcoming one, in Katherine's opinion.

"Have you any dances spare, Lady Katherine?" Timothy ventured.

Katherine twisted up her dance card to look, and he craned his neck to see.

"I do believe I may have secured the final dance, my dear fellow," Lord Barwood said, his voice pointedly jovial.

"No, no, I have a few slots spare," Katherine said, trying not to let her heart sink at her packed dance card. She'd barely have a chance to breathe between sets, let alone rest.

"I see you're quite busy," Timothy said, his voice quiet. When she glanced up, his eyes were resting on the dance card. "Dancing all night is a tiring thing, I'm sure. Perhaps you'd like to rest a little."

"Yes, thank you," Katherine said, not quite able to hide her relief. That wasn't kind, was it? Feeling relieved that she didn't have to dance with her brother's oldest friend.

Timothy smiled at them both, made a tight bow, and slipped away, leaving Katherine with Lord Barwood again.

"A quiet sort of chap," Lord Barwood observed. "I daresay he'll spend the whole evening melting into the background, hiding in corners and watching people."

"He's always been a good friend to William, but I can't say I know much about him. Oh, I do hope he's not offended. It's just that this is our first hosted party since... since the funeral."

Lord Barwood looked suitably sympathetic. "I am sorry. But your older brother is growing into his role as the new duke, I've heard."

"Yes, he's doing an excellent job."

"I wonder, could I fetch you some punch, and perhaps find us a couple of chairs?"

Something fluttered in Katherine's chest, and she snatched at it eagerly. What was this feeling? It was new. Was it attraction?

Well, why not? He was a handsome man, a charming one, and he was clearly interested in her. He knew her father, which wasn't exactly a mark in his favour, but it did mean that he was known to the family. She needed to find someone, after all.

Before Katherine could respond, however, the musicians started up with a flourish. Couples started to take to the dance floor, chattering eagerly, pairing up. William materialized from nowhere. He looked pale and tired but kept a brave smile on his face.

"Ah, it's Lord Barwood, is it not? A pleasure," he said, in the voice that Katherine recognized as his Society voice, level and measured, with a hint of enthusiasm but not too much.

"Yes, indeed," Lord Barwood responded. "I'd engage you in conversation, but I suspect you've come to claim your dear sister for the first dance."

"I certainly have. Are you ready, Katherine? The ball won't open without us."

William offered his arm smilingly to Katherine, who took it, glancing back at Lord Barwood as she did so.

"I look forward to our dance, Lady Katherine," he said, making a bow. "I do hope you won't forget."

"As if I could," she said, laughing, and William drew her away.

"He seems nice," William remarked, under his breath. "You've gone all red."

"Have I?" Katherine's hand flew up to her face. "He came up to me and introduced himself, you know."

"Shocking. Don't let Mother know."

"I won't, I'm not a fool. Did you speak to Timothy tonight?"

"Only briefly, I'm sorry."

William clicked his tongue. "He's too reserved for his own good. I do worry about him. He... he knows about the business of the will, by the way."

Katherine stiffened. "What? Why did you tell him?"

"I trust him completely, Kat. In fact, I have more faith that he'll keep the secret than I do that Henry will."

She shifted uncomfortably. "Perhaps so, but I don't like him knowing that sort of thing about us. Still, he's your friend, and I suppose Timothy is a good sort."

"He certainly is. I've put him next to you at dinner. Do talk to him, won't you?"

"I'm hardly going to ignore the person who sits beside me at dinner, am I?" Katherine muttered. She was conscious of a feeling of disappointment, now that she knew for sure she wouldn't have Lord Barwood beside her at dinner.

Stop it, she warned herself. *Don't get in too deep too soon. This is a mercenary business, no point pretending it isn't.*

Still, this was a promising start, was it not?

Katherine and William took their places at the head of the set. Glancing down the set, Katherine noticed plenty of familiar faces. She saw her friend, Lady Elizabeth Morrison, was standing up with a genteel-looking man. Elizabeth was plumply pretty, with a sweet round face and vivid red hair. She caught Katherine's eye and smiled, and Katherine made a mental note to speak to her later.

Henry was standing up with an older-looking lady – some dashing widow or another – and Alexander was leading out a white-gowned debutante, who seemed to be afflicted with a fit of nervous giggles.

"They're all dancing. That's good," William murmured. "But that Mrs. Harrison is simply not suitable, I'd better warn Henry away."

"That sounds like the ideal way to get Henry to propose to her immediately. I should let them get on with it, if I were you. What about you, Will? You saw me talking to Lord Barwood – and he seems pleasant, at least – and Henry and Alexander are being proactive. What about *you*?"

"I've talked to everybody and nobody tonight," William muttered. "I have to greet everyone or else they'll take offence, and that means I haven't time to conduct a proper conversation with anybody. A host of hopeful mammas have introduced me to their daughters, nieces, and so on, and I daresay when it's time to choose a bride, I can pick one."

"Don't talk about choosing a spouse as you would choosing a biscuit," Katherine objected. "For all we're being forced into it, marriage is *serious*. I want to marry for love, Will."

Her brother smiled sadly at her. "Oh, Kat. You still believe that you can, don't you? I think perhaps it's time to grow up a little, don't you?"

Before Katherine could respond to that, the music started in earnest, and they were obliged to start dancing.

Chapter Four

Timothy was not dancing. Of course he wasn't dancing. Dancing would require having to ask a lady to dance. For a gentleman like him – nice and personable enough, but with few prospects, a *second* son who was known to live in a shabby apartment – ladies would not exactly be queuing up to get his attention.

Perhaps it was for the best. His dancing was serviceable, but not exactly elegant.

Lord Barwood, on the other look, looked like some sort of fairy prince. He moved elegantly around the dance floor, with Lady Katherine in his arms. Was this the third dance of the evening, or the fifth? Timothy had lost track. The dances started one after another, with very little pause for breath, and the couples clashed and milled around on the dance floor between each set, entering or leaving the dance floor, looking for their next partners.

"I thought I might find you here," said a familiar voice, pushing through the crowd to stand at Timothy's elbow. "Why are you not dancing, Timmy?"

He smiled faintly down at his aunt. "Please don't call me *Timmy* in public, Aunt Amelia, I beg you."

Miss Amelia Spencer was somewhere in her thirties, a confirmed spinster, but hardly *old*. She lived with her sister and brother-in-law, Timothy's parents, and had all but raised her two nephews and niece. She had never been considered *pretty*, not in the way her older sister was *pretty*, and Timothy had always thought that unfair. Miss Spencer had a round, kindly face, which could be described as plain if a person was particularly cruel, and had dull brown ringlets kept back with a ribbon and done up in a simple style. She was warm and friendly, and had been described as 'maternal', which was likely intended to be a compliment. She had lived with her sister and brother-in-law since the death of her parents, which came only a few years after her older sister's marriage.

Timothy had wondered, more than once, whether his aunt really was content with her life. If she wasn't, she never let on. Now, he slipped her arm through his, and gave it a gentle squeeze.

"*Timothy*, then. I forget that nickname is only for at home."

And not even then, Timothy thought grimly. The only people who still used his childhood nickname were his aunt, and occasionally his younger sister. Speaking of which...

"Are Rebecca and Christopher here tonight?" he asked, as casually as he could. "And Lord and Lady Rustford?"

"*Lord and Lady Rustford*," Amelia repeated, with a snort. "Would it be too much trouble for you to refer to them as Mother and Father?"

"Father said it's more proper. You are aware of his strict adherence to propriety and politeness."

"Yes, I do know." There was an edge in Amelia's voice, and he didn't risk pushing any further. "No, none of them are here tonight. They received invitations, of course, but they're all dining with Constance's family tonight. My attendance was never particularly important, so Arthur decided that I should come here on behalf of the family."

Timothy pressed his lips together. "Yes, that sounds like something Father would do. He always had a penchant for sending people here and there at a whim. You're entirely too obliging with him, Amelia."

"May I remind you that I live in your parents' house at the good-will of my sister and her husband? Not everybody longs for freedom as you do, Timothy."

"Did," he corrected. "I have my freedom, now."

Amelia said nothing. "Well, you've successfully avoided my question. Why are you not dancing?"

"I don't feel much like it."

"No? I had it on good authority that you were going to ask Lady Katherine to dance."

Timothy flushed, biting his lip. He should have known better than to try and keep a secret from his aunt. She was famous for knowing everything that went on in Society, and had a knack for excising and keeping secrets.

"I was," he said, as neutrally as he could, "but her dance card was all but full already."

"Hm. Which was it, then? Full, or all but full? There is a difference, you know."

"There were spaces," he clarified, "but she'll be exhausted if she dances every dance. I would be unkind to insist. It's not as if a lady can refuse to dance with a gentleman."

Amelia gave a snort. That, at least, was true. For a lady to refuse to dance with a gentleman was quite a shocking event. It generally happened a few times every Season, with some over-confident debutante or desperate young woman finding herself in an unbearable situation. A lady refusing an offer to dance would find herself obliged to refrain from dancing for the rest of the night, regardless of how full her dance card might be. It was a tremendous humiliation for everybody involved.

"You are too kind, Timothy. Do you think Lord Barwood over there refrained from asking her to dance to save her feet getting too sore? No, I think not."

Timothy pursed his lips. "I'm sure I'm more thoughtful than Lord Barwood. How do you know him?"

"Oh, the whole town is talking of him. He's recently returned from the Americas. He's tremendously wealthy, naturally, and excessively charming and handsome into the bargain. Half a dozen mammas at least have their sights set on him for their girls. It seems to me, though, that he has his mind set on his own prize."

She nodded towards the dance floor, where Lord Barwood and Lady Katherine were promenading together. As Timothy watched, Lord Barwood said something to make his partner laugh.

Something tightened in Timothy's chest, something sharp and a little painful.

"I'm glad she's having a good time," he said firmly. "I imagine there hasn't been much to make her laugh since they lost the Duke."

"Hm, if you say so. I don't believe he was a remarkably good father. But let's not speak ill of the dead. Do you know, the

Willoughby boys have all danced every dance tonight? That's unusual. I know for a fact that Henry hates dancing, and William avoids it when he can."

Timothy bit his lower lip until he tasted copper. He knew, of course, why the boys were all dancing. They needed to find marriage mates within the next year or go through life penniless.

"I daresay they want to make a good impression," he said lightly, careful not to look at his aunt. "It is their first ball for a while, after all."

The music ended with a flourish, and the dancers stopped, laughing and clapping. Couples bowed and curtsied to each other, all smiles, subtly mopping sweat from brows and necks.

No new song began, as there would be a break now for supper. The dancing would resume afterward, when everybody's supper had settled a little.

Timothy spotted William taking his leave of his partner, a pink-faced debutante whose mother was already coming to claim her back. He made a beeline straight for Timothy and Amelia.

"Hello, you two," he said, out of breath and smiling faintly. Not a real smile, Timothy noticed. It didn't quite reach his eyes. "Timothy, you're sitting next to Katherine at supper. I hope you don't mind, we just wanted friends around us. Miss Spencer, you're beside him. Would you mind escorting Katherine in to dinner, Timothy?"

That tight feeling returned to Timothy's chest. Would she be disappointed? Was she hoping that the handsome and charming Lord Barwood, who was dripping in confidence and never at a loss for something to say, was the one who'd escort her in?

It didn't matter. His friend was asking him.

"Of course," Timothy responded. "I'll find her at once."

The guests formed into pairs and loose trios, snaking lazily through the emptying ballroom towards the dining room.

For his part, Timothy had been here many times. The long, imposing, highly polished dinner table was an acquisition of the late Duke's. Often, instead of clustering his family around one end as a normal family would do, he insisted on everybody spreading out. The Duchess would sit at one end, he at the other, the four children spread halfway down each side. It successfully killed all but the most vital conversation and left each person feeling alone and entirely cut off.

That, of course, was likely the intention.

Glancing down at the woman on his arm, Timothy wondered whether Lady Katherine remembered these meals. He had no doubt that she did.

"Are you enjoying yourself, Lady Katherine?" he asked quietly, as they queued to get into the room. It felt appropriate to say something. He didn't want her to think she was sitting next to some foolish, dull old clodhopper.

You're a writer. Can't you summon any words?

"Oh yes, very much," she said, not entirely convincingly. "My legs ache terribly. I haven't danced so much in at least a year."

"Ah, I see. You can rest tomorrow, can't you?"

"Yes, I can, but that doesn't do a great deal for my feet right now."

"No, I suppose not." He cleared his throat, racking his brain for another subject.

"I meant to thank you, by the way," she said suddenly, almost giving him a start.

"Thank me? What for?"

"You declined to ask me to dance because my dance card was already full. You said I ought to rest, didn't you? That was very considerate. Thank you, Mr. Rutherford."

A lump formed in Timothy's throat. "It's no trouble at all, Lady Katherine. I think your brother would be upset to know that I made you dance without rest."

She chuckled wryly, and there was an edge to her voice. "Oh, William has far too many things on his mind to worry about me being tired. Have you seen Henry, by the way? He trod on Mrs. Eversham's gown during the last dance, and she's most angry."

Timothy winced. "I have not seen him, I'm sorry."

And then they were in the dining room, a cavernous space with the soft murmur of muted conversation rising up to the ceiling, and it was time to concentrate on finding their places.

Timothy was a little surprised to find himself so near the head of the table. He caught William's eye, who was just lowering himself into the host's place. William looked pale, with dark circles under his eyes. Katherine did, too, their olive skin barely brushing the edge of *sallow*. He spotted Alexander further down the table, sitting between a widow and her debutante daughter, chatting to them both. There was a notable gap opposite, with two bored-looking ladies on either side.

Timothy glanced down at Katherine, who was also staring at the empty space, a muscle jumping in her jaw.

"Henry has taken himself off," she murmured. "I shall scold him later. For now, there's not a great deal any of us can do. He's a grown man and can't be dragged by his ear to the dinner table. Not that I don't wish I could."

They all sat, and the first course was served. It was a thin soup, a *consommé*, designed to whet the appetite without filling up a person. Then there would be course after course of lamb and fish, good roast beef, duck, bread and vegetables, fruit, both sugared and ordinary, delicate sweetmeats, marzipan, trifles, cakes, and so on. Far too much food for anyone to eat, even with the number of guests at the table. Genteel conversation drifted along, all very polite and uncontroversial.

Timothy spotted the exquisite Lord Barwood, looking a little petulant between a portly lord and a severe-looking reverend. Lord Barwood was looking at them – or rather, looking at Lady Katherine. Timothy didn't have to glance down at her to know that she was looking back.

"So, Lady Katherine," he said, dipping his spoon disinterestedly into the *consommé*. "I feel as though we haven't talked in an age. Longer, perhaps."

She smiled wryly. "Not since our dear papas stopped being such good friends. The late Duke did not allow us to visit you, and vice versa. I recall William saying that he could only see you at the club."

Timothy bit his lip. "Yes, I recall. Let's be glad those days are over."

"I agree. I hear that you have apartments of your own, now?"

"Yes, I do. Nothing very fine, but I enjoy my freedom."

She nodded, and thankfully did not ask him how he made his living. Would that be a vulgar subject for the dinner table or not? Timothy couldn't recall. The rules changed constantly, and there were a host of taboo subjects there were appropriate or inappropriate in various settings. It was exhausting.

I miss my study, he thought miserably. *I miss my Rosalie.*

Immediately, another thought followed it, this one hitting his chest like a physical blow.

Your Rosalie is not real, fool.

"You read a great deal, don't you, Lady Katherine?" Timothy managed.

"Yes, but nothing very improving. My unfortunate parents were nearly pulling their hair out in distress. I would barely even read poetry – it was all novels."

"There is nothing wrong with novels," Timothy said, laughing.

She shot a quick glance at him. "What a refreshing outlook!"

He lifted an eyebrow. She was not looking at Lord Barwood now.

"Refreshing? How so? I was of the understanding that everybody reads and enjoys novels."

"Oh, they do, make no mistake. However, it's incredibly *gauche* to admit that one likes novels. One must pretend to find them silly and over-dramatic. One must repudiate the sentiments and excess romance found in such books. One must pick apart the writing, and tear the plot to shreds, and claim that one found the heroine far too silly and nonsensical."

She rolled her eyes, and Timothy found himself laughing.

"You speak from experience, I think."

"I certainly do. Why must reading be *improving*? Why can a person not read simply for enjoyment?"

"Ah, there we do not agree. I believe that all reading *is* improving, regardless of the subject. I don't believe a person can read a book and find themselves more foolish at the end of it.

Enjoying a story is never a waste of time and being enthralled by a set of characters and a plot – no matter how ridiculous – will always be improving. In my opinion, that is."

"Very cleverly put," she laughed. "I'll try and remember that next time somebody complains about my choice of novels. For such a quiet man, Mr. Rutherford, you have quite a way with words."

To his horror, Timothy felt colour tinging his cheeks. Blushing like a schoolgirl, how ridiculous.

No, he thought, suppressing a smile despite it all. *Blushing like a heroine.*

"I take it you read novels yourself?" Lady Katherine asked.

"Oh, yes, although I haven't read one in some time, I'm afraid. Not since Mrs. Radcliffe's last publication."

"Oh, I adore Mrs. Radcliffe. I read the last volume of *Udolpho* in one sitting."

"Goodness, how admirable."

"For myself," she said, reaching for her wine glass, "I have just finished the most wonderful novel. Perhaps you've heard of it – *Rosalie's Trials*? I have just finished the second volume, and I simply cannot wait for the third. I wish the wretched author would release all the volumes at once."

A tingle ran down Timothy's spine. His hand shook where he held his soup spoon, and he laid it down so as not to disgrace himself.

"I'm familiar with the book," he managed. "The third volume is coming along slowly, I've been told. You... you enjoyed it?"

"Enjoyed it? I adored it. Rosalie is exactly the sort of heroine every novel should have. I quite loved her. I cannot wait to find out what pickle she'll get herself into next. The author is remarkably talented. L. Sterling, that is their name. It's said to be a pseudonym, of course. I've read all of their novels."

Timothy swallowed hard. "All of them? Even... even *Marianne*? That was said to be something of a flop."

"Oh, I don't think so. It didn't reach the same heights of success of Rosalie's adventures, but it was a remarkable book, nonetheless. The first novel I read was *The Lodger of Addam House*, and the ending made me cry so hard I thought I should die."

Timothy gave a nervous laugh. "I imagine the writer cried themselves, writing that ending."

"I hope so, the wretch. You've read those books too, I take it?"

"I have read them all," Timothy said, before he could think to make a more cautious answer. "I've read them all countless times, each and every one."

She shifted in her seat to face him properly, her expression bright.

"It's so good to find a fellow admirer of L. Sterling!"

He smiled weakly. "I'm not sure *admirer* is the word."

Chapter Five

It was hard for Katherine not to let herself be swept away by excitement. Rules were rules, and she had to remain restrained and decorous at the dinner table, no matter how eager she was to talk about L. Sterling with Timothy. Who would have thought that quiet, sweet Timothy would have known so much of her favourite novels! The man had an almost encyclopedic knowledge of the characters, of the plots, of the themes that were explored!

The minutes slipped away, and the chatter and noise around them simply vanished.

"I disagree entirely," Katherine said, at one point in the conversation. The desserts were being served now, and she couldn't quite believe that a dinner like this – usually so tedious – had flown past so quickly. "Lord Marlborough is certainly a villain, of course, but he does have good qualities. He cares for his mother so completely, and really, the poor man only wants to be loved. He isn't right for Marianne, of course, and they would never be happy together, but I should dearly love to read another book about him. A book about his redemption, of course. Perhaps a more forthright woman would suit him better. Somebody a little older, a widow or confirmed spinster perhaps."

"I have to wonder," Timothy said archly, "whether you'd be quite so forgiving of Lord Marlborough's wickedness if he wasn't so handsome."

"Oh, probably not," Katherine laughed, feeling a little giddy. "But he is *compelling*, nonetheless, and he doesn't do anything *too* evil. Some of my companions who read the same book agreed."

"Perhaps you're right, but I can assure you that Lord Marlborough was simply created as a villain, and a rather flat one at that."

"How can you possibly know that?"

Timothy choked a little on his wine. "Well, I rather assumed. Just my opinion, of course."

She nodded, leaning back in her seat. The meal was almost over. Soon, the Duchess would rise, and that would be the signal for them to rise too, engaging in light conversation and various polite antics until their suppers had settled enough to dance again. The ladies and gentlemen were not splitting after the meal today, which was quite a scandalous choice which would be talked about a great deal.

Still, they would likely get away with it. Katherine knew from experience that Society would forgive anything that was bright and pretty and entertaining enough.

Don't be so cynical, she reminded herself. *If all goes well, you'll have to engage with Society in order to get yourself a husband. If you don't marry, we're all doomed.*

On cue, the Duchess rose, looking wan and pale in her black silk. Everyone had spoken to her, of course, to pay their respects and exchange pleasantries, but nobody had stayed very long. Katherine almost felt sorry for her mother.

Before she could think on it, Lord Barwood appeared behind her.

"Lady Katherine, I trust you enjoyed your meal?" he said, smiling. "Before the dancing begins and I lose you again, perhaps you'd care to take a turn about the room with me? The dear Dowager Duchess mentioned that there are a great many portraits in the Great Hall. Could I request a small tour?"

Katherine waited for the fluttering feeling she'd felt before, but it didn't come. Lord Barwood's smile was just as charming as before, but nothing. Maybe it was all the food sitting heavily in her stomach, and the lingering knowledge that Lord Barwood almost certainly wouldn't have the same interest in novels.

"Of course," she said, as if there was any other response to give. She turned to Timothy, who was now standing awkwardly behind his dining chair, not quite looking at either of them. "Do excuse us, Mr. Rutherford."

Timothy gave a neat bow and a smile. "Of course. Have fun, please."

He met her eye, just for a minute. He had green eyes, Katherine noticed. She knew, in a disinterested sort of way, that Timothy Rutherford *did* have green eyes, but suddenly, they seemed even more vivid than usual. Had he always had streaks of gold in them?

Then Lord Barwood cleared his throat, and Katherine blinked as if waking from a reverie.

"I'll see you later, I'm sure," Katherine said, smiling. "Goodbye, Timothy."

It was only as they were walking away that she realized she'd used his first name, which of course was entirely inappropriate. Even if he was one of her brother's closest friends.

*****

The sun was rising by the time the last carriage rattled away down the drive.

Katherine stood by the doorway with the boys, waving. At least, with William and Alexander. Henry had been unaccounted for during most of the night, and had at some point taken himself off, whether to a club, an artist's gathering, or bed, she wasn't entirely sure.

Lord Barwood had been one of the last guests to leave, and had said his goodbyes slowly, with many smiles and hand-kisses.

Alexander was leaning against the wall, yawning, while William stood with his back straight at the doorway, not quite ready to abandon his host-persona.

Timothy had left sometime earlier in the evening. He hadn't said goodbye, although perhaps she'd been too engrossed with Lord Barwood to notice.

"Katherine?" the Duchess materialized at her elbow. "I'd like a word, before you go to bed."

It wasn't much of a request. Katherine was exhausted, naturally, but she'd gotten to the stage of tiredness when she felt strangely numb and disconnected, almost as if she were floating along the halls, following her mother's black silk train rustling around corners.

The Duchess led the way to the morning room she used for her own personal use. A fire was lit, crackling merrily, warming the room and the rising sun filled the room with light.

She closed the door firmly.

"I noticed you making an effort with Lord Barwood," the Duchess said, in the tremulous, quiet voice she'd adopted since her husband's death. "He's an eminently suitable man."

Katherine bit her lower lip. It felt odd, talking about marital prospects with her mother. Before the late Duke passed away, the matter of his children's marriages had been his decision. It was very clear that he would have the final decisions on who they would marry, and when. Had the Duchess even cared? Katherine could easily have believed not.

"He was very charming," Katherine managed at last. "He made an effort with me, too."

"You danced with a great many gentlemen, all entirely suitable. And your brothers all chose their partners wisely. Except for Henry, of course, who seemed intent on choosing the most ridiculous ladies to dance with. Spinsters, widows, and so on, all entirely unsuitable. You must have a word with him."

Katherine clenched her jaw. "Yes, Papa used to think I ought to marshal my brothers, too. He didn't believe I could do anything right, but somehow, I ought to be able to do that."

The Duchess pressed her lips together, but admirably did not rise to the bait.

"Lord Barwood had business dealings with your Papa," she said instead. "He thought well of the man. He said that he had great potential and had achieved much for one so young. I think he would be pleased at the idea of a match between Lord Barwood and you."

That doesn't make me like him more, Katherine thought. She was glad she wasn't quite tired enough to say this out loud.

The Duchess had never been a strong woman in any way, but she was more diminished now than ever. Some days, she seemed so wan and colourless that it seemed she would disappear eventually.

"I haven't made any decisions," Katherine said, when it became clear that a response was required.

The Duchess pursed her lips and took a tentative step forward.

"It would make me very proud if you made a match with a man like Lord Barwood," she said, reaching out a tentative hand. Her fingers were cold on Katherine's arm. She didn't pull away, but after a moment, the Duchess limply took her fingers away. "I was proud of you tonight. Of all of you. You looked remarkably beautiful."

Katherine stared at her mother. She'd wanted, so badly, to hear that before. She'd wanted to hear her mother say that she was proud of her, for whatever reason, even if it was only for her looks.

And now here it was, and she felt nothing. Was it too late?

"I'm tired, Mama," Katherine heard herself say. "I think I'd better go up to bed. I'm sure Lord Barwood might visit tomorrow. Or today, rather. I keep forgetting that it's *today* now. Elizabeth is coming today as well."

The Duchess made a little *moue*. She'd never much approved of Elizabeth as a friend for her daughter. The late Duke certainly hadn't, but now William was the Duke, and Katherine could choose her own friends.

"Goodnight, Mama."

Katherine turned without waiting for a reply and hurried along the lightening hallway towards the stairs. She wanted nothing more than to go to bed but had a strange feeling that she wouldn't sleep very well.

***

"It was an absolute triumph," Elizabeth gushed, leaning forward to help herself to another small cake, one of the leftovers from last night. "Everybody said so. Did you read what the gossip column said about it?"

"No, I didn't."

"Shall I read it out to you?"

"Please, Lizzie, do *not*."

The ladies sat together in one of the smaller, informal parlours, mid-afternoon, drinking tea and enjoying cakes. The party atmosphere of last night seemed very far away.

Elizabeth was wearing a lemon-coloured gown with orange polka-dots, a rather bold shade and pattern. Katherine had always admired that about her friend – she stuck to her own style, preferring bright, jaunty colours to the pastels of the Season. Elizabeth was never going to be considered a Beauty, but nobody in the city had a bad word to say about her. And some of them had tried, certainly.

"What did you think of Lord Barwood?" Katherine asked, after a pause.

Elizabeth considered, swilling her tea around her cup. "He's very handsome."

"Yes, he is handsome. But what else?"

Elizabeth pursed her lips. "Well, I don't know, it's not as if he spoke to me."

Katherine flinched. "Why not? Why wouldn't he?"

Her friend cast her a sympathetic look. "Gentlemen often don't, Kat. I'm not as pretty as you."

"Why should that matter?"

"It does matter, and you know it. Let's not talk of that right now. You danced with Lord Barwood twice, that's rather scandalous."

"It's not scandalous so long as we don't dance together twice in a row," Katherine chuckled. "Come on, who did *you* dance with?"

Elizabeth winced. "Well, I didn't dance *much*. I did dance with Timothy Rutherford, though."

The prickles ran down Katherine's spine again. "With Timothy Rutherford? I didn't think he was dancing."

"Oh, he didn't. Not much, at least. But we were talking – he *is* a pleasant gentleman – and I think we were both rather bored. I know this will shock you, but I asked *him* to dance, can you believe it? We were in a quiet corner, and I guessed he wouldn't be the man who'd swoon at it. So, we stood up together. It was quite thrilling, I can tell you."

Katherine bent her head, pouring out another cup of tea. "Do you think you'll make a play for him?"

"Don't be so mercenary, my dear, it doesn't suit you. Now, *I* want to hear whether Lord Barwood has called on you."

"No, not yet," Katherine said, adding a lump of sugar. "I'm sure he will, though. He left his card here this morning."

"Do you think you'll make a match with him?" Elizabeth asked, eyeing her over the rim of the teacup.

"Oh, goodness, I don't know. I barely know the man. He is rather nice, though. He's rich, and so am I. Or so I will be, when..." she faltered, her sentence trailing off, and Elizabeth thankfully didn't press for an answer. They sat for a moment or two, sipping tea in companionable silence.

"Mother wants me to marry," Elizabeth said, matter-of-factly. "You know my parents spoil me terribly, of course, but there's no getting around the fact that I'm hardly a debutante, and I must get married, sooner or later. This Season is rather my deadline."

"Mine, too," Katherine admitted. "I just... I just worry, that's all. What if I pick the wrong person?"

"You'll have more choices than me," Elizabeth pointed out wryly.

"Let us separate the wheat from the chaff of the Season together, eh? Oh, before I forget, I must tell you something I learned last night. Timothy Rutherford is an admirer of L. Sterling."

That made Elizabeth sit up straight. "Oh, really? I know plenty of gentlemen who read Sterling's novels, but they rarely admit it."

"Yes, I sat next to him at supper, and we talked about it the whole time. You know, I've known Timothy Rutherford for years – at a distance, of course – and I never knew he enjoyed novels so much. He made the evening very pleasant, when I wasn't dancing off my shoes. Speaking of which, my feet still hurt."

Elizabeth chuckled. "I must know, Katherine, are you serious about marrying this Season? Only, you've never seemed too keen on marriage before."

Katherine swallowed hard. "I think perhaps it's time for me to settle down."

"Hm." Her friend eyed her closely, and Katherine pretended not to be catching her eye.

Not yet, she thought. *I haven't the strength to go through it all again.*

There was a strange sort of atmosphere in the house at the moment. In the days after the funeral, when they were free and didn't know the final insult their father had prepared for them, there'd been a vibrant, happy atmosphere. Not at all the sort of atmosphere one should have after a death in the family.

But they'd had hope, had hoped for their future lives to be happy and safe, free from their domineering father.

And then the will had been read, and that was that. This time next year, if all went well, they would all be married. There would be four new in-laws to consider, and Katherine herself would have a husband.

Ugh.

Katherine swigged down the last of her tea with a sigh.

"My advice," Elizabeth said, seriously, "is to avoid the fortune hunters and gentlemen with obvious intrigues attached to their names. Aside from that, there's no way to tell the good ones for the bad ones. I know plenty of ladies who married gentlemen they thought were good and kind, and they ended up miserable and neglected. You can never tell."

"Thank you, Elizabeth," Katherine snorted. "That's very encouraging."

"Well, one must learn the truth sooner or later. Now, let me see which gentlemen left their cards."

"By all means have a look," Katherine chuckled, gesturing to a little silver platter of neat cards. She expected visits from most or all of the owners of the cards, probably by the end of the week. Most were gentlemen she'd danced with, along with ladies who had hopes of one or several of her brothers and intended to further the acquaintance with her in order to achieve this.

It was going to be an exhausting week or so.

"Oh, Timothy Rutherford left his card with you," Elizabeth said, holding it up. "He's the second son, you know, so his marital prospects won't be so terribly good. I don't believe he has a great deal of money. I wonder how he makes a living?"

"I'm sure he gets an allowance or something similar." Katherine leaned forward. She hadn't looked through the cards properly and hadn't noticed that Timothy had left one. Why? He wouldn't need to leave a card. They were all acquainted, and they were already friends, more or less. She twitched the card out of Elizabeth's hand, turning it over. She smiled, shaking her head.

"He's left a smudge of ink in the corner. See, there? It looks like a fingerprint."

"Oh, lord," Elizabeth laughed. "Just as well he left it here and not somewhere else, he'd be laughed out of London."

"I'm sure there are more terrible crimes than leaving a smudgy card," Katherine remarked.

She sat back in her chair, still holding the card. It was a simple one, ever so slightly bent, as if he'd just pulled it out of his pocket, and that idea made her smile for some reason. She could see Lord Barwood's card from here, a gilt-edged thing with graceful, elegant script.

She held onto Timothy's card. It would be nice for him to call again. They could talk about novels again. However, it was more to the point if Lord Barwood called – after all, he was probably the one she would end up marrying.

Chapter Six

Meetings with his editor – Mr. Hawthorne – were already stressful. Knowing that his deadline was looming, and the book was nowhere near ready did not make Timothy feel any better. It was clear that Timothy was not in the editor's good books, judging by the amount of time he'd been kept waiting in the stuffy, dusty foyer.

The spotty-faced clerk who could be no older than nineteen appeared in the doorway.

"Mr. Rutherford?" he asked, officiously. "You can come in now, if you like."

Timothy shuffled into the familiar, cramped office, with faded and cracked green leather armchairs, stuffed with books, and a desk overflowing with papers angled away from the window. Mr. Hawthorne was a man in his forties who'd gone grey prematurely, probably after dealing with his host of writers. His hair stuck out around his head like a halo, and he had bushy grey eyebrows to match.

He stared at Timothy over his half-moon spectacles with an air of resignation.

"I'd hoped that you would have had more of the book completed by now, Mr. Rutherford."

Timothy settled into the seat opposite, and grimaced.

"It's coming along, Mr. Hawthorne, I assure you."

The man grunted, indicating that he was not assured in the slightest.

"Is what I've given you not enough?" Timothy asked, nodding down at the sheaf of papers on Mr. Hawthorne's desk.

"This is a summary, along with a few sections. It will do for now, but I'll need something more for editing, of course. I've already highlighted some issues."

"Oh?" Timothy felt a niggling feeling of dread in his stomach. This was not a good start. When he'd provided the manuscript for his first ever book, and his first volume of *Rosalie's Trials*, the editor had gushed over it, adored it, and been dying to read more.

Now, Mr. Hawthorne was looking at him with the sort of severity a schoolmaster would direct towards a schoolchild presenting an inadequate essay.

"I felt that Rosalie was not quite so... *tangible* as she was in the earlier volumes," Mr. Hawthorne said. "Have you had any issues while you were writing?"

"Issues?"

"Yes, personal issues. In my experience, a writer who has something on their mind tends to write... well, differently. The readers will notice."

Timothy bit his lip. "Oh, I see."

"You're not obliged to explain yourself to me, naturally. What I've read so far is not *bad*, but you do have a great many dedicated readers with high expectations. *Is* everything alright?"

"Well, my parents are pressuring me to marry, as usual," Timothy said, trying to give a light laugh. It didn't come off quite as casual as he intended. "They want me to marry an heiress, since writing hasn't made me rich."

The family did not know that Timothy was L. Sterling. They knew he wrote novels under a pseudonym and had never bothered to inquire further.

Mr. Hawthorne flashed a sympathetic smile. "Difficult, I'm sure. Now, let's discuss your deadline..."

"I'll have it finished in time, Mr. Hawthorne."

He received a flat and disbelieving stare. "I'm sure. Well, here are some notes I made on the story so far. My advice to you, is to find Rosalie again."

Timothy gave a snort. "I wasn't aware I'd lost her."

Mr. Hawthorne leaned forward, resting his elbows on the desk.

"A writer might lose sight of their characters when something else is occupying their own minds. For example – not that I say this is your problem, naturally – a woman. That can be all very well, but it can impact writing one way or another. Perhaps if there is a lady you have in mind, you could resolve matters before finishing *Rosalie*. Just a suggestion, of course – I don't presume to direct you in how to write, naturally!"

"Naturally," Timothy echoed, forcing a quick smile. "Is there anything else? I have a family dinner to attend."

"Ah, how lovely."

It certainly is not, he thought, but forced a sickly grin onto his face.

***

Rustford House was more like a castle than anything else. It had been in the Rutherford family for centuries and was a large and imposing building. Designed in the years when space was paramount over comfort, Timothy's bedroom had been larger than the entire apartment he lived in now.

And yet he knew exactly where he'd rather be.

The craggy, cadaverous butler greeted him at the door, grim-faced and unsmiling. Timothy unceremoniously stripped out his coat, gloves, and hat, and bustled along to the drawing room to greet the rest of his family.

As he approached, he heard the high, nasal sound of his sister-in-law's laughter.

Constance was there already, then. Wonderful. The Rustford family did not need money, exactly, but Constance was a tremendously wealthy heiress of excellent birth, and as such, she was a suitable match for Christopher and was therefore welcome into the family.

The fact that she was thoroughly unlikeable and shallow did not matter in the least.

Timothy paused before the door, drawing in a deep breath and straightening his waistcoat. Then he pasted a smile on his face and went in.

The family were arranged as usual. Everybody had their seats, and those seats were to be stuck to.

Lord Rustford sat in a huge, winged armchair by the fire, the family's chairs arranged around him in a semicircle. Lady Rustford had a suitably smaller chair on the opposite side of the fire, with a stool for Aunt Amelia. A long sofa was provided between them, for Christopher, Constance, and Rebecca.

Another chair could be pulled up for Timothy, when he arrived.

They all glanced up when he entered.

"Ah, he deigns to grace us with his presence at last," Lord Rustford said heavily.

Constance cackled again, and Christopher beamed indulgently at her.

"Well, I'm glad you're here, Timmy," Rebecca said, bouncing to her feet and hurrying over to hug her brother.

Timothy was well aware that he didn't much resemble any of his family. Lord Rustford was a tall, portly man with grey blond curls and a perpetual frown. Lady Rustford was a flimsy, faded woman who had never been seen to smile. Christopher looked like a younger and stupider version of his father, and Constance had been blessed with wealth but not beauty, and certainly not charm. Rebecca was pretty, everyone said so, but was entirely too reserved and unsure of herself.

That was likely due to her overbearing and judgmental family. The only thing they had in common, in Timothy's opinion, was the green eyes that they all shared, except for Lady Rustford and poor Aunt Amelia.

A chair was duly produced for Timothy, and he sat down. Heavy silence descended, like a blanket of thick snow over a field. The clock on the mantelpiece ticked steadily, reminding them all of how long they still had to go until they actually sat down to eat.

"So, Timothy, have you thought any more of giving up that ridiculous apartment and coming back home?" Lady Rustford said, after the pause became almost physically painful.

Lord Rustford snorted. "What makes you think he'd be welcome, my lady?"

Timothy clenched his jaw, aware of Constance and Christopher tittering together.

"Thank you, Mother, for the kind offer, but I'm quite settled." He said, as politely as he could manage.

"Well, I miss you," Rebecca said stoutly, then quailed under a stare from Christopher.

More silence. Silence was the norm in the Rutherford household, unless Lord Rustford had something to say.

"Since we're all here," Christopher said, glancing sideways at his wife, "Constance and I have something to say."

"Well, make it quick," Lord Rustford rumbled. "I don't much like heavy conversation before dinner. My lady, call the butler and have dinner brought forward. I'm tired of waiting."

Christopher drew in a breath and got to his feet. Beside him, Constance smoothed out her skirts and smiled expectantly around at them all. A flash of intuition started up in Timothy's gut.

"Well, Constance and I have been married for well over two years now, and we have some news of a happy, *happy* event," he said, in a well-rehearsed way. Lady Rustford gave a genteel little gasp and clapped her hands over her mouth.

Christopher savored the moment -as was his custom- and lingered indulgently.

"We're expecting a baby," he finished, beaming around.

There was a half-second of silence, then everybody was on their feet, surging forward to the happy couple.

"Well, that's excellent news, my boy," Lord Rustford said, grinning. "It's high time we had an heir in the family. You're making your father very proud."

Rebecca and Aunt Amelia smiled and fussed over Constance, who was smiling shyly and ducking her head with false modesty. Lady Rustford held back, smiling tightly and remaining in her seat.

Timothy tried to catch Christopher's eye, intending to offer congratulations. Lord Rustford was clapping his older son's shoulder, the very picture of restrained paternal affection. They both glanced Timothy's way at the same time, and he was perfectly placed to see their expressions turn cold and contemptuous.

It was not a pleasant thing to see. He swallowed hard, shuffling forward and offering a hand.

"Congratulations, Christopher," Timothy said, with forced joviality. "This must be very exciting for you."

Christopher sniffed. "Well, one of us needs to do their duty for the family."

There was a taut silence after that, broken neatly by the butler appearing at the door.

"Your lordship, your ladyship, dinner is served," he intoned.

"Shall we go through?" Rebecca said, in a none-too-subtle attempt to change the atmosphere in the room.

"I for one am starving," Constance announced, rising gracefully to her feet and placing her hand on her stomach. "After all, I'm eating for two now."

This received indulgent smiles.

"You all go through," Lord Rustford said suddenly. "I would like to speak to Timothy for a moment."

There was no way, no way at all that this was going to be something good. Timothy swallowed hard, stepping aside to let the others trail past him. Lady Rustford sailed past, barely sparing a glance for her disappointing second son. Aunt Amelia laid a comforting hand on his shoulder, and Rebecca risked a smile up at him. Christopher and Constance did not look at him at all.

And then they were alone, the door was closed, and the silence fell even heavier over the room.

Timothy waited, heart pounding, his hands tucked behind his back. He didn't dare sit again – Lord Rustford would take it as an insult, a sign of disrespect.

The vast carpet in front of the fireplace, easily larger than Timothy's living room at home, stretched between them. Timothy twined his fingers together, pressing hard enough that his nails would undoubtedly leave crescent moon marks on his flesh, and waited.

After all, the great Arthur Rutherford, Lord Rustford himself, would not be rushed.

To prove a point, Lord Rustford inspected Timothy for an endless moment, then turned and made his way leisurely across to the whiskey decanter in the corner. He poured out one tumbler, and took a careful sip, savouring the flavours. Timothy clenched his jaw until his teeth squeaked.

"Excellent news about your brother," Lord Rustford said at last.

"Yes," Timothy managed. "I know that Constance and he have wanted a child for some time. I'm glad for them."

Lord Rustford smiled tightly. "Yes, although they have been married for two and a half years, and this is the first sniff of baby so far. It may not even be a boy. I'm sure you can see how that may present a problem. There may be no more children."

Timothy swallowed. "Yes, but for now, they're celebrating. We're celebrating. The baby may be a boy, and then even if they don't have more children…"

"An heir and a spare," Lord Rustford interrupted.

Timothy fell silent. As he'd suspected, this conversation was taking the direction he'd thought.

"That has been the rule for centuries," his father continued, "And for good reason. Life is uncertain. Accidents happen. Illnesses come. For a great house and estate like ours to survive, we must always be looking to the future. And by that, I mean children. Heirs. Christopher did his duty at once, marrying an eminently suitable woman, and now they may produce an heir. Rebecca is unmarried, and so, my boy, are you. This must be remedied with all speed."

He swallowed hard again. His mouth was dry. He hadn't been offered so much as a cup of tea since he entered. Even now, the family would be in the dining room next door, staring at the dinner which Lord Rustford had insisted should be put on the table earlier, unable to eat a morsel. At least they'd have water and wine within reach.

"I never expected," Lord Rustford spoke again, slowly making his way across the room towards his son, "that you should make as marvelous a match as your brother. But I did expect that you would make a *suitable* one. And now here you are, unmarried, writing… writing *novels*, living in hovel."

"I live in a perfectly respectable apartment, Father."

"Do not contradict me. Where is your future? Do you intend to live as..." he paused, lip curling, "... as *L. Sterling*?"

Fear arced through Timothy, seizing up his muscles and all but rooting him to the floor with dread. Lord Rustford ventured a sly smile at his expression.

"Ah, you thought I did not know? Very sweet. You should know by now, my boy, that I know all things. I found out right away what your pseudonym was. If you must write novels, I intend to keep a tight rein on what you write. If you had not moved out of the family home, I would have long since put a stop to it all."

"But I have moved out of the family home," Timothy managed. "You pay me no allowance, and I have never asked for money. I support myself. I haven't attempted to disgrace the family by revealing my identity. What have I done wrong?"

"I think I have been clear," Lord Rustford said crisply, throwing back the last of his whiskey, barely tasting it. "I do not object to your novel-writing, since you have had the sense to choose a pseudonym. Your writings are immensely popular. I have never read any, of course, but I daresay they are passably good, if one enjoys popular modern trash."

Timothy smiled grimly. "Do you know, Father, I think that's the closest thing to a compliment I have ever heard from you."

Lord Rustford did not, it seemed, like that. His head jerked, and his eyes narrowed.

"Do not disrespect me, boy. Do you think I can't reach you? You think that moving out of your home and disgracing yourself as a scribbler puts you at a safe distance? Oh, no. If I applied myself, I daresay that no volume of L. Sterling would ever grace the shelves of a bookseller's again."

"You say that," Timothy responded, taking a step forward and trying to swallow down his anger, "But my novels are popular. Very popular. I make money for myself and for others. Are you quite, *quite* sure that you can make people forget?"

Lord Rustford smiled thinly. "Would you like me to try?"

Timothy stopped. The answer, simple and poignant, was *no*. He thought of the tired Mr. Hawthorne, the shabby publishers, and the ladies and gentlemen who were not rich, buying his books.

What could his father do about it? Timothy was not entirely sure, but one thing he did know.

Lord Rustford was a man who would stop at nothing for revenge. No act was too cruel, no retribution too heartless.

"What are you saying, then?" Timothy managed, after the pause had stretched out between them. "Are you blackmailing me? Am I to toe the line and do as I am told, and marry the lady you pick out for me, or else you will sabotage my career and kill my novels? Is that it?"

Lord Rustford gave a hoarse, mirthless laugh. He set down the empty whiskey glass with a *clack* and withdrew an expensively embroidered handkerchief to dab at his lips. This, too, was part of the act, designed to make Timothy feel more uncomfortable and out of place with every passing second, more likely to blurt something out or lose his nerve.

"Don't be so dramatic, you ridiculous boy," Lord Rustford scoffed. "Blackmail and arranged marriages, good heavens. I never heard the like of it. It's clear you're a novel-writer. Those books are full of lunacy, from what I've heard, and nonsensical situations. Why anyone would want to fill their heads with that, I could not say. No, I do not intend to blackmail or force you into a marriage. I do, however, expect you to act more like the gentleman that your position requires. You think that leaving home and turning up your nose at an allowance and my money frees you of responsibility, do you? You'll find it otherwise."

"So, you want me to marry?" Timothy said, pleased that his voice did not shake. Not much, anyway.

"You should think about it," Lord Rustford said decisively. "An heir and a spare, boy, an heir and a spare. Now," he clapped his hands together, indicating that the conversation was over. "Let's go in to dinner. They'll be waiting."

Timothy followed his father mechanically. There wasn't much else to do, really.

Chapter Seven

"Morning, Mama."

The Duchess glanced up at her daughter, thin lips curving into a smile.

"Good morning, Katherine. Might I say, you were a remarkable success at the ball. Every scandal sheet comments on it the last two days."

A tingle ran down Katherine's spine. She seated herself at the breakfast table, trying not to look at the newspapers and scandal sheets spread out over the surface. Her mother read them all, naturally, memorizing key bits of gossip as if there would be a test on them later.

There was no sign of Henry and Alexander, but William sat at the head of the table, turning over the pages of a ledger, his breakfast mostly untouched. He looked exhausted, she thought.

"I always thought those scandal sheets were written for the purpose of inciting gossip and causing a stir, rather than conveying any actual information," she observed. "Don't you think so, Will?"

A vague grunt was her only response.

"You ought to read them, dear," the Duchess said severely. "They can be a good indication as to whether Society is accepting you or rejecting you."

"The writers of those rags – anonymous, all of them, which I think is very telling – only care about provoking commotion. That is all."

The Duchess tutted. "Well, take a read of this here. Go on, read it."

Pressing her lips together, Katherine pulled the thin magazine towards herself and began to read, albeit reluctantly.

She would be lying if she said she didn't feel pleased, just a little.

Success!

This is the word on everyone's lips regarding the mysterious and beautiful Lady Katherine Willoughby. Emerging from mourning rather too soon for propriety's liking, the handsome and charming Willoughby siblings have nonetheless created a real stir in Society. Lady Katherine was resplendent in a colourful gown, in excellent looks, with her dance card full of notable names.

The ball itself was remarked upon favourably by all attendees, demonstrating the famous hospitality and hosting skills of the Willoughby family, and the great charm of Lord William Willoughby, the new Duke of Dunleigh.

In fact, all four Willoughby siblings are creating a great stir on the Marriage Mart. This author thinks that a great many eligible ladies and gentlemen will be looking the Willoughby way after last night.

Despite herself a flush rose to Katherine's cheeks. Praise was praise, even if it came from a scandal sheet rag with an anonymous author.

"Well," she said, as coolly as she could. "That is quite complimentary. I'm glad people seem to have enjoyed themselves at our party."

Despite intending not to read further, Katherine glanced down at the page again, and her name appeared again. Almost without thinking, she began to read again.

Lady Katherine Willoughby was also seen dancing with the handsome and well-liked Lord Geoffrey Barrington, Earl of Barwood. Are wedding bells ringing out for this good-looking couple? The author thinks so. A match between Lord Barwood – handsome, rich, charming – and Lady Katherine – beautiful, freshly out of mourning – would be a fine match indeed. Beauty, wealth, and charm on both sides of an engagement? Why, is that not the aim of every lady and gentleman venturing out into the marriage mart? We shall watch these two lovebirds with interest.

Flushing, Katherine shoved away the paper.

"Well, that's nonsense, for a start," she said brusquely. "These authors have no right to matchmake like that. I have no intentions of marrying Lord Barwood."

"Oh, don't be ridiculous, Katherine," the Duchess scoffed. "Of course you do. You'd be a fool not to consider it. He's an entirely suitable match, and he's paid plenty of attention to you. Don't tell me you haven't thought about it."

Katherine bit her lip. She had thought about it, of course she had. But to read it here, laid out in black and white for the whole world to see, was another matter entirely.

"The whole of Society will be watching us now," she said bitterly. "They as good as announced our engagement. I'm not pleased about this, Mama."

"Well, there's nothing you can do about it," the Duchess retorted sharply. "And that's that."

Before another word could be said, the butler stepped into the dining room.

"Lord Barwood for Lady Katherine, your ladyships, your lordship," he said demurely. "I have shown him into the parlour, as his Grace informed me that he was expected."

Katherine shot William an appraising look. He avoided her gaze.

"Thank you, Mr. Ruth. I'll be along shortly. Bring in tea, won't you?"

He gave a bow and departed.

Katherine glared at William again. "Thanks for the warning, Will."

She got to her feet before he could respond, sweeping out of the room. Best to get it over with, she supposed.

***

Lord Barwood was standing by the window when she entered, turning with a smile. She had to wonder whether he'd chosen the spot deliberately, with the light shining around him like a halo. It was a flattering light, too.

"Ah, Lady Katherine," he said, smiling. "I was half-expecting to find you still abed, after the chaos of the party, even if two days have already passed."

She smiled. "No, not at all. Please, take a seat, Lord Barwood."

He did so, and there was a half-minute of awkward silence before Ruth appeared, bearing the tea-tray. That allowed them to delay conversation for a few minutes more while the tea was taken care of.

"I was wondering," he said, when tea was poured and biscuits doled out, "what time you would like me to pick you up today?"

She flinched. "I beg your pardon?"

His self-confident smile wavered a little. "To promenade, of course. In the Park? I have a fine new gig I'd like to show off, and it's a fine opportunity to get some air, eh? It's been a while since I promenaded during the fashionable hour. It'll be pleasant, I thought."

There was a taut silence.

Is this his way of asking my permission? Asking if I'd even like to promenade? He's simply assuming, Katherine thought, with a flinch of annoyance.

Promenading was, in her opinion, ridiculous. It wasn't about exercise, taking in the beauty of the Park, or even simply socializing. It was about being seen, about looking good and fashionable, about *being*. About showing off a new gown or a new gig without seeming to show off.

"I... I am not fond of promenading," she said slowly.

He blinked, seeming taken aback. "Oh. Well, the Duke never mentioned that. He said you'd be delighted to come out today."

For a split second, Katherine imagined her father, the Duke. She stared at him, bewildered, full of questions.

And then she remembered. The Duke was dead, long live the Duke.

"Oh," she said hesitantly. "You mean William."

Lord Barwood frowned. "Well, yes, of course I meant William. Who did you think I meant? I asked his permission first, naturally. Promenading is a remarkably public thing, is it not?"

She pressed her lips together.

"And he gave his permission on my behalf, did he?"

"Yes, yes he did." Lord Barwood seemed relieved now, almost satisfied. He drank his tea in one long gulp. "So, shall I call back after luncheon?"

"Not today, I think," Katherine said shortly. "I'm sorry, Lord Barwood, would you excuse me for just a moment? I need to speak with my brother about something."

"Oh," Lord Barwood blinked. "Is everything alright?"

"Of course. Please, finish your tea and biscuits. I believe there's cake, too. I do beg your pardon."

She got up without another word and strode out of the room before he could say anything.

***

"Care to explain why you told Lord Barwood he could take me promenading today?"

William, leaning over more ledgers on his desk, flinched at her voice. He glanced up at her, guilt in his eyes. Katherine folded her arms tightly across her chest.

"Well?"

"Don't be like that, Kat," he muttered. "Lord Barwood asked to take you promenading. Look, I have tickets to that play you like, *Much Ado About Nothing*. It's playing in the Theatre. I thought you'd enjoy it, and it would make up for promenading with him. I *tried,* Kat. He asked me directly, put me right on the spot. W hat was I meant to say?"

"You were meant to say that you would ask me first, not make a decision on my behalf without even *consulting* me. Better yet, you should have told him that I'm my own person, living and feeling, with my own thoughts, and he should ask me himself. And then I would have said no, because I hate promenading."

William sat back in his seat with a sigh. "Can you truly not see why I'm concerned? All of us need to marry, myself included. Father saw to that. For the rest of us, it only concerns ourselves whether we choose to claim our fortune or not, but *all* of us are reliant on your marriage to even have the opportunity. You can't pretend that your decision only affects yourself."

"And I don't," she shot back, pulling out a seat and throwing herself into it. "But please, William, let me manage this matter myself."

"Like it or not, I am the Duke."

"I never said you weren't."

"I don't just have the title. I *am* the Duke. Everything you do reflects on me. I am responsible for taking care of Mother, of you, of Alexander, of Henry. My responsibility. Mine. That means that I have to ask questions, take charge, get involved."

"Take *charge*?" Katherine echoed. "I hope you don't intend to be like Father, trying to control everything we think and feel."

"Of course I don't. I couldn't, even if I wanted to, and I *don't* want to. But I want to be involved, Kat. Don't you think it's fair for me to want that?"

She bit her lip, passing a hand over her face. Suddenly she felt unbearably tired, even though it was barely past breakfast.

"Don't make any more decisions on my behalf, William," she said shortly. "Even if you think they're for the greater good. I want you to promise."

William clenched his jaw. "Kat..."

"Promise, Will! I know I need to marry, for everybody's good. I know it, and I intend to do my duty. But I need to manage this myself. I *must* manage it myself."

He pressed his lips together in a tight line. "I promise, Kat."

She exhaled. "Good. That's good. That's all I wanted to hear. Now I have to go back to the parlour and tell Lord Barwood I won't be promenading today."

"Kat..."

"Not *today*, Will. That's all I ask."

She got to her feet, smoothing out her dress with a shaking hand.

If I'm going to have to marry Lord Barwood after all, she thought miserably, *I'm going to do it in my own time.*

Chapter Eight

William watched Katherine go. He felt shaken, and more than a little guilty.

She was right, he shouldn't have answered on her behalf. He didn't particularly like Lord Barwood, but he was an eligible suitor, and he was handsome. He'd paid attention to Katherine and seemed the most likely to make an offer. And in the end, that was the most important thing, wasn't it? Whoever would make an offer.

For himself, William could ask a different woman to marry him every week until one said yes, but Katherine was obliged to wait and hope. And, as he kept reminding himself every hour of the day, until Katherine married, they were all doomed to pennilessness.

A penniless duke, he thought miserably. *How ridiculous.*

He eyed the ledgers and papers spread out on his desk, full of figures. None of it was particularly appealing, but the work had to be done.

He was the Duke now. If he didn't do it, nobody would. He would be expected to act a go-between for Katherine and Lord Barwood. If Lord Barwood wanted to marry her, he'd ask William's permission first, as was the protocol. He suspected she wouldn't like that.

But it was his *responsibility*. If Katherine never married, if Alexander and Henry's behaviour got more shocking, if the family money drained up, it was *him* that would get the blame. In society's eyes, and, he thought, in his family's too.

A tap on the door made him jump.

"Who is it?"

The Duchess peered around the door. In the past few months, she seemed to have retreated into herself, getting paler and weaker. The prospect of organizing weddings for her children, in rapid succession, had brightened her up a little. Thank heavens for small mercies.

"I happened to overhear what Katherine said to you," she said crisply.

He sighed. "Because you were listening at the door, no doubt."

"Gentlemen do not accuse ladies of eavesdropping, William. But that is beside the point. You must assert authority with her."

He flinched at that. It was almost as if his father was in the room again, stone-faced.

Women need a strong hand, my boy. Children, too. One can never be weak. One can never relent, not even for a moment.

He shuddered. "Katherine is a grown woman, Mother. She knows what's at stake, and she'll do her duty. I don't want to interfere in her life more than necessary."

This was not what the Duchess wanted to hear. She pursed her lips.

"Well, when Katherine has a husband, *he* will interfere in her life as much as he sees fit. She will have to get used to it."

"Then she had better choose wisely." He responded sharply.

I really must stop thinking of Mother as the Duchess. *When I marry – and marry I must – my wife will be the Duchess.*

There was another tap on the door, and the butler appeared, looking nervous.

"Your Grace? Lord Alexander is home. There is… there is a matter that needs your attention. Lord Henry requested that you come at once, and only you."

Tension prickled down William's spine. A series of worst-case scenarios, each one more horrible than the last, swirled through his mind.

"Where is he?"

Alexander was sprawled on his back in a narrow hallway, tucked behind the kitchen and pantry.

"I brought him in through the back door," Henry said, leaning against the wall. "None of the servants saw. I didn't think you'd want him to be seen in this state."

"You're right about that," William muttered. "What, is he drunk?"

"Absolutely."

On cue, Alexander waved a hand faintly, making a gurgling noise. William groaned.

"Push him onto his side. If he vomits now, he'll choke on it."

"Do it yourself," Henry said, voice sharp.

William blinked at him, a little taken aback by the tone. Sighing, he stepped forward, shoving Alexander onto his side.

"Where did you find him?"

"A truly foul little pub in a side street. You'd have been shocked, truly. He didn't even have enough money to pay for his bill. I paid it, and I want the money back, by the way."

At first, William thought he was joking. Crouched beside Alexander and listening to his snoring, he glanced up. The smile faded from his face when he saw Henry's expression.

"You're serious."

"Of course I'm serious," Henry had his arms folded tightly, his expression impassive. "I don't have money to waste on paying a fool drunkard's bills."

William bounced to his feet. "We're not talking about a fool drunkard! This is your brother! And, might I add, Alexander would do this for you in a heartbeat."

"I'd never put myself in such a situation," Henry took a step forward. "You'd have been ashamed of him. He couldn't stand, let alone walk. I had to all but carry him home. He vomited twice, and nearly got him. And it wasn't even good alcohol. It was just the nasty, cheap stuff. Disgusting. He stinks of it, must have poured half a cup down himself." Henry wrinkled his nose, and William took a step backwards.

It was something of a shock, seeing such anger on his brother's face.

"It's not Alexander's fault we're in this predicament."

"I didn't say that it was. But you're the one who said we had to make the best of it. Do you think that *this* is making the best of it?"

He gestured angrily at Alexander, who was now blinking sleepily, looking pale and queasy.

"Oh, I got home. Good."

William felt a surge of irritation. What *was* Alexander thinking? He was the youngest of them all, meant to be the one who was sensible and kind and caused no trouble. And yet, here he was.

"Don't let Katherine see him in this state," he muttered.

Henry rolled his eyes. "Do you think that I would?"

"Frankly, I don't know with you at the moment, Henry. I just don't."

"And what's that supposed to mean?"

The brothers squared up to each other, arms folded, glaring. William felt unsettled, as if his skin were too tight, the sense of unease he'd been feeling all day intensifying.

What has that wretched will done to us all? He thought despairingly. *We never hated each other so much before.*

"It's supposed to mean that you've been distant and unfriendly, acting as if you're the only one suffering. Do you really think we're thrilled about being forced into marriage? Do you think Katherine is pleased to find our entire fortunes resting on her shoulders? Do you think a ticking clock hanging over our heads makes us feel safe and happy? Do you, Henry?"

Henry shook his head angrily. "I was *happy*, Will. Really, truly happy, and it was all just wrenched away from me. At least being here, you were all used to being miserable."

William flinched at that. "How can you say that? What are you even saying – that we're used to it, so it shouldn't bother us anymore? We were going to be *free*, Henry. We were so happy. And then it was all wrenched away. At least you got to be free for a while. You got to travel."

Henry shook his head violently. "I'm not going along with it. I'm not going to stay here and shop for a wife. No, I'm leaving."

William hadn't been expecting that. He blinked, staring. "I... you're going to leave? You can't leave."

"Of course I can," Henry retorted. "Why shouldn't I?"

"You won't get your inheritance."

Henry shrugged. "Well, it would be better than marrying someone simply to get my hands on Father's money. I reckon it would the best revenge, don't you? Show him that I'm not dependent on him. That I won't play his game."

William held his gaze for a long moment, then groaned, raking his hands through his hair.

"Oh, Henry. Look, I can't prevent you from doing what you want. And I wouldn't want to. I'm not going to be that kind of Duke."

Some of the anger melted out of Henry's face. He looked, all of a sudden, younger, more like the little brother William remembered.

"I'm not leaving right away," he muttered. "Just eventually. I won't up and go without warning, if that's what you mean."

"Are you two fighting?" came a hoarse, gurgling voice from the floor. They glanced over to where Alexander lay. He was awake now, albeit a little disoriented looking.

"It's nothing to worry about," William said firmly. "We're just tense, all of us."

Henry mumbled what might have been an agreement.

There were noises coming from the kitchen, and William was fairly sure that the servants would be along soon.

"Come on," he said firmly. "Let's get him upstairs and into bed, shall we?"

Henry grumbled, but obediently grabbed one of Alexander's arm. Together, they hauled him into a standing position, and began to drag him towards the servants' stairs.

"I know I shouldn't have drunk so much," Alexander said later, as they were manhandling him into bed. "'I am sorry, Will."

"It's fine," William sighed, pulling off Alexander's boots. "Just don't make a habit of it, eh?"

"It's just... just the ball, you see. I tried my best, I tried so hard. I danced with everybody I could, I was as charming as possible, and I just felt... I just felt nothing. And don't get me wrong, the women I danced with were all perfectly pleasant. They were pretty, and intelligent, and seemed to enjoy spending time with me. And yet I felt *nothing*. I was waiting for that feeling they talk about in books. I was *ready* to fall in love, so that when Katherine gets married I could get married right after, and we'd be set for life, my wife and me. But I felt nothing. That's when I realised how it was going to be."

"And how's that, Alex?"

Alexander squeezed his eyes closed, swallowing hard.

"I'm not going to fall in love. I'm just going to have to choose someone, aren't I? Choose someone or lose my inheritance. So will Henry. It all seemed so pointless. So, I went out and drank until I couldn't stand up. Silly, isn't it?"

William bit his lip. He wanted to say something comforting, of course, but there was nothing really to say.

For starters, Alexander was right. If he didn't fall in love before the year was up, he would face a choice – marry somebody anyway, or simply forfeit his inheritance.

"All that alcohol is making you maudlin." He said firmly. "You'll feel better in the morning, I promise."

"It is the morning, you absolute fool."

"Ugh. Later today, then. Sleep through luncheon, and just pray that you'll sleep tonight."

Alexander smiled tiredly. "Good night, then. Good morning, rather."

William slipped out of the room, closing the door softly behind him.

***

Lunch was a somber affair. Katherine was clearly in a bad mood after the business with Lord Barwood – which William acknowledged was his fault – and the Duchess had got to hear of it, so *she* was in a foul mood, too.

Alexander was naturally still in bed, and there was no sign of Henry. Of course not. Mr. Ruth had announced that he had left shortly after Alexander got settled. There was no talk of Alexander's inebriation, thankfully. Maybe it could be swept under the rug and forgotten.

That would be William's duty from now on, wouldn't it? Sweeping things under the rug.

He swallowed hard, his cold chicken suddenly sticking in his throat.

"You won't find a better man than Lord Barwood, you know," the Duchess said suddenly, a clear sign that she'd been thinking it over during the painfully silent lunch. "You're a fool if you think otherwise."

"I haven't turned him down, Mama," Katherine responded shortly. "There was no proposal. I simply won't be promenading with him today, that's all."

"You ought to encourage him now, young woman. You are a lady, and so you had better not take too much for granted. It's alright for William – he's a duke, so he can marry whoever he likes."

William flinched. "Perhaps I want somebody to marry me for something more than that."

There was a taut moment of silence after that. Katherine shot him a quick, searching look.

"Of course they will. You're a wonderful man, William. Besides, we wouldn't allow you to marry somebody who just wanted the Duke of Dunleigh," she said slowly, as clearly as she could. "Would we, Mama?"

The Duchess made a little *moue*. "Young people these days are far too sentimental about marriage. It's a matter of business."

"And affection has no place in it?" Katherine shot back immediately. "I hope for a marriage that is based on more than *business*."

"You ought to moderate your expectations immediately, my girl," the Duchess snapped. "Because if you do not marry, we'll be thrown into poverty, all of us. Far too much rests on you. I don't know what your father was thinking, leaving it all on your shoulders. I always thought he was an intelligent man who knew the measure of his children, but now I think otherwise."

Katherine threw back her chair, leaping to her feet. She stared down at her mother for a long moment, then turned on her heel and marched wordlessly out of the room. The Duchess stared after her, then followed, leaving William eating alone.

He sat in silence for a moment or two, staring at the now unappetizing-looking mess on his plate.

Once again, the attention had been neatly directed from him to Katherine. Not that he resented it, of course. It just felt that the only time anybody ever paid attention to William, the oldest, was to find fault.

He did not have the luxury of going abroad and recanting his fortune, like Henry planned to do. He did not have the luxury of drinking himself silly and worrying about love, like Alexander. He had to marry. The Duke of Dunleigh could not be penniless. He couldn't afford to lose his portion of the fortune, and therefore he simply could not afford to let Katherine go unmarried. The sooner she was married, the better for them all.

It was not going to make him popular with the others. Katherine's chances of getting a good match relied directly on how properly her family behaved. If Henry was acting surly and aloof, and Alexander getting drunk and playing the fool, Katherine's prospects would suffer.

And so, the responsibility for making them behave rested squarely on William's shoulders.

For himself, he'd better look around for a suitable lady, someone to marry as soon as possible after Katherine's marriage.

He never imagined for a moment that he would find love. Plenty of women would want to be the Duchess of Dunleigh, and that was the best he could hope for. William was not a man who threw his heart open wide at the slightest flash of feeling – his father had knocked that out of him early on. There was no time to try and pry his heart open.

Well done, Father, William thought, with a surge of bitterness that tasted as sour as bile in his mouth. *You've made us just as miserable now that you're dead as we were when you were alive. Congratulations. Wherever you are, I hope you're satisfied.*

Chapter Nine

"I can't believe you've never seen *Much Ado About Nothing*, Becky," Amelia laughed, twitching back the carriage curtain to look through the window. "When I was young, I saw it all the time. It was – and is, I believe – Timothy's favourite play."

Outside, the rain was beginning to fall, and dusk was coming on. Not that it mattered – even from here, Timothy could see the bright lights of the Theatre beckoning them forward.

The carriage moved slowly, weaving its way through the crowded streets. *Much Ado* was one of the more popular plays, with plenty of comedy and likeable characters, and he had no doubt that the theatre would be packed tonight. Ordinary people with just enough money for a standing ticket were filing into the main auditorium, while ladies and gentlemen of a higher standing would be escorted to their reserved boxes.

Occasionally, Timothy had deliberately bought a standing ticket, and pushed his way through the crowded floor, solely to experience it for himself. It was a thrilling experience. Crowded, to be sure, as well as hot and bothersome, but he *felt* the play in a way he hadn't quite before, experiencing it breathlessly with hundreds of others, elbow to elbow. It was a worthwhile experience and had served as the basis for one of his hero's scenes in *Northwood Castle*.

The carriage jolted to a halt at last, before the wider, neater entrance for 'proper' ladies and gentlemen.

A theatre attendant came forward to open the carriage door and pull down the steps. Amelia and Rebecca climbed down almost together, chattering excitedly, leaving Timothy behind.

He didn't mind. He followed, smiling to himself, watching his aunt and sister lean on each other, happy without the cloying presence of the Rutherford family. He was glad he'd offered to take them today. It would be a good thing for them both.

And then the two ladies stopped so suddenly he nearly walked into their backs.

"Oh," Rebecca exclaimed. "Lady Katherine is here!"

Timothy's heart plummeted into his stomach, his good mood evaporating immediately. He glanced past the two women, and sure enough, there she was.

Lady Katherine looked breathtakingly beautiful tonight. She was wearing a pale blue gauzy dress with long white gloves, a delicate white lace shawl around her shoulders. That shawl was currently being taken by none other than Lord Barwood himself. Of course. He assiduously folded the shawl, handing it unceremoniously to the maid accompanying her mistress.

Lady Katherine looked... well, it was hard to identify her expression. She kept a pleasant smile on her face, of course, but the smile seemed fixed in place, and did not reach her eyes. When Lord Barwood reached out to take her arm, she flinched, almost imperceptibly. Steeling herself, she accepted his arm with a gracious smile, and the pair turned to leave the foyer and find their seats.

"Wait!" Rebecca called, louder than a lady was meant to speak in public, making them all jump. "Lady Katherine!"

The woman in question turned, and Timothy was perfectly placed to see relief and happiness spread across her face.

"Miss Rutherford! Lady Amelia!" she exclaimed, slipping her arm away from her escort and hurrying towards them. "How excellent to see you! Can I assume you are going to see the Shakespeare play, too? *Much Ado* is one of my favourites."

Lord Barwood was obliged to follow Lady Katherine, although he looked rather displeased about it all. Lady Katherine swept her eyes over Timothy, sparing him a small smile which made him feel oddly nervous, then returned her attention to the two women. Lord Barwood gave him a brief nod, and that was all. No matter, though. Timothy was happy to stand and be quiet. They formed a little group in the foyer, chattering happily between themselves.

And then – miracle upon miracle – Rebecca discovered that they were, in fact, all sitting in the same box.

Lord Barwood looked almost comically annoyed, and Timothy fought to suppress a pleased smile.

Up in their box – number twenty-four – the entire theatre spread out below them. Candles glittered everywhere, uncountable, and Timothy found himself wondering who had the responsibility of lighting all of those candles each evening and putting them out afterwards. A novelist had to consider these details, even if they were never written down. Books, as everyone knew, were not simply paper and binding. They were stories, and stories ran deeper than black print on white paper. Much, much deeper.

Their box was comfortable, affording a good view of the stage. Talking amongst themselves, the ladies took the seats closer to the balcony, leaving Lord Barwood and Timothy to sit behind.

And then Amelia hesitated, glancing behind her.

"Wait, Timothy, take my seat. It's not fair for you to sit behind, it's your favourite play."

"No, Amelia, I'm fine."

"I insist," she said firmly, getting up and gesturing to her empty seat. "You let me sit in the best seat when we went to see *Hamlet*. It's only fair."

And so, Timothy found himself sitting between Rebecca and Lady Katherine, with Amelia and a disgruntled-looking Lord Barwood sitting behind with the maid. His skin became covered in goose-flesh.

Stop it, he scolded himself. *Concentrate on the play. Have you never sat next to a pretty woman before?*

It wasn't just any pretty woman, though. It was Katherine Willoughby, the woman who'd occupied his thoughts for longer than he could remember.

The heavy velvet curtain on the stage undulated, indicating that it would be raised soon. The chatter in the audience dimmed just a little, expectantly.

"It's been far too long since I saw this play," Lady Katherine remarked, voice low. "I'm as excited as a child."

"So am I," he responded. "This is Rebecca's first time seeing the play."

"When I first read L. Sterling's book, *Roses for Violet*, I was shocked at how strongly Violet resembled Beatrice. You know, the character in the play. Everybody's favourite."

"Ah, yes, the witty heroine," Timothy managed. It still felt odd, hearing his own books and characters so casually mentioned. "I believe she was based on Beatrice."

"Yes, it seems that way," Lady Katherine laughed, and he was able to recover himself and his slip-up.

There was a comfortable pause, not the tense silences Timothy was used to around his family and some acquaintances. It didn't *feel* like a silence. It felt as though there was plenty of them to say, but neither of them was in a rush to say it.

"You understand them so well," Lady Katherine blurted out, after a minute or two, almost as if she'd been waiting to say it. "The L. Sterling books, I mean. Have you really read them all?"

Timothy swallowed. "Every single one. Sometimes I think I can recite them in my sleep."

"So do I," Katherine laughed. "I remember the very first book I ever read by that author. There was something fascinating about it, something breathless and *real*. Some authors seem intent on getting a moral across, and some of the male authors seem to enjoy making their poor heroines suffer. *The Monk* was one of those books. I couldn't finish it; it was too awful."

Timothy winced, recollecting the book in question – full of assaults, unspeakable crimes, and suffering. He'd read in it in full, after his editor suggested he do so, and it had left him with a bitter taste in his mouth. Mrs. Radcliffe's works, on the other hand, were a little more palatable.

"I feel as though the author does have a message they want to convey," he said slowly. "All of the main characters – heroes and heroines – are not permitted to be passive. They make things happen. They make mistakes, too, but the mistakes are their own. They take responsibility for what they have done, too."

"Like Pierre La Blondeville," Katherine interjected eagerly. "His arc of redemption was truly compelling. I couldn't put it down.

But I do think that his acceptance of his own crimes, and the way he did penance, made the difference between we readers forgiving him or not."

"Yes, I imagine that was what the author intended," he responded, allowing himself a small half-smile. "If I were to guess, I would say that good old Pierre was one of the trickiest characters that author ever wrote. I can almost imagine the editor haranguing the poor author, insisting on endless edits."

"Oh, Timothy, you are funny," she said, laughing. "As if any editor would dare to nag L. Sterling. Why, the author is one of the most famous of our era! No editor would dare contradict them. Having said that, I imagine the publishing house is getting nervous over the length of time it's taking for the final *Rosalie* book to be released. We're all on tenterhooks, wouldn't you say? I for one can't wait to find out what happens next."

Timothy, who had every line of the third book's plot engraved on his head, smiled nervously. He was still reeling from the implication that his editors would not dare nag him – a sentiment Mr. Hawthorne certainly did not share – when Lord Barwood leaned forward, a heavy hand landing on Timothy's shoulder, making him jump.

"I do hope you two aren't going to whisper throughout the whole play," he muttered, the smile on his lips not quite reaching his eyes. "If you persist in distracting Lady Katherine, Mr. Rutherford, I'll have to insist on us swapping seats."

The large hand on his shoulder flexed, fingertips driving painfully into Timothy's skin. He suppressed a wince.

"My apologies, sir," he responded brusquely. There was a flourish of music, the curtain began to rise, and Lord Barwood was obliged to sit back and be quiet.

Timothy had seen the famous Shakespeare play so many times he could almost recite each line.

"I would rather hear my dog bark at a crow, than a man swear he loves me," insisted fiery Beatrice, while her sweet cousin Hero hid her smile behind her hand.

"Let me be as I am, and seek not to alter me," spat the villainous Don John, who Timothy had always rather sympathized

with – the man was clearly chafing under his half-brother's reign, although he didn't exactly help his own case.

"*I do love nothing in the world so well as you,*" Benedict murmured, at the climax of the play, when Hero was disgraced and her cousin Beatrice sitting crumpled on the edge of the stage. "*Is not that strange?*"

When Beatrice shouted out, "*O, God, that I were a man! I would eat his heart in the marketplace,*" the theatre rang, and he heard Lady Katherine's breath catch in her throat.

Wasn't that the way every woman felt when her friend, her family member, had been hurt, and she found herself helpless to defend them. He could not imagine the simmering rage, the endless depths of fury a woman might feel at a time like that.

Glancing over Lady Katherine, who was intent on the stage, eyes glittering, lips parted, he could almost see her – a bloody, still-beating heart in her fist, its blood seeping down her arm and staining her face, a dead villain lying at her feet.

Then he blinked, and the moment was gone, the scene was over, and the next one was beginning.

Lady Katherine leaned towards him, close enough to brush their shoulders together.

"That particular scene always has the power to stir within me a shiver of intense emotion," she admitted. "I can't hear it often enough."

"I agree," he responded. "I think Claudio should think himself lucky Beatrice was not a man – or at least, didn't get her hands on him. I'm not sure he would have lived to make amends with the woman he spurned."

Lady Katherine nibbled her lower lip. "I think if I were Hero, I wouldn't have taken him back. Oh, I know that she had no choice, and that she was likely happy enough with the way things worked out. But how could she ever trust him again? Without trust, there can be no love."

"Perhaps so, but love is more than emotion. It's principle, isn't it? One decides to love as much as one *does* love. And Hero, for all her faults as a character, was exceptionally loving."

Lady Katherine considered this for a moment and nodded slowly. "I think perhaps you're right."

Then Lord Barwood cleared his throat pointedly behind them. He'd spent most of the first acts yawning mightily, but now was taking offence to a little whispering. Suppressing an eye roll, Katherine straightened up, returning her attention to the stage.

She shot Timothy a quick, knowing look, and heat filled his chest. Smiling weakly back, he tried to pay attention to the rest of the play.

***

The play was over. Applause had been given, lots of it, and the actors had come out and made their bows. People were leaving. Far below them, in the pit of the theatre, the ordinary folks were fighting chaotically around, trying to get to the exits, talking and laughing and shouting. The boxes were a little more orderly, with finely dressed men and women taking their time, enjoying genteel conversation, no doubt discussing where to go next.

Timothy, of course, would be going home. He would drop Amelia and Rebecca off at the family home, and then return alone to his apartments, which would be dark and silent, waiting for him.

He half turned to Lady Katherine and caught her looking at him. There was something odd about her gaze, something thoughtful and... was that wistfulness? If only he could read the faces of real people like he could his characters. Real people were complicated and never did what they were supposed to do.

"I enjoyed the performance very much," Lady Katherine said, her voice dipped as it had been during the play, as if she were speaking to Timothy and Timothy alone. Her voice spread over his skin like water and wasn't *that* a curious image.

"I... I did, too," he managed. "I thought that..."

"I'm surprised you heard a word of it," came Lord Barwood's firm, crisp voice, "with all the chattering you two did."

Lady Katherine's expression smoothed out into the Society mask so many ladies adopted. She flashed a quick, tight-lipped smile up at him.

"On the contrary, Lord Barwood. I heard every word."

The man smiled tightly. Timothy suspected that he did not like to be contradicted. He was ignoring Rebecca and Amelia entirely, and barely spared a glance for Timothy.

"Well, my dear, I think we had better be going, don't you? After all, we want to keep up your strength for tomorrow. We will be promenading together," he added to Timothy, not quite able to keep a smug smile from his face.

Timothy nodded, keeping his expression blank. A lady and gentleman – unrelated and unengaged – meant only one thing. An interest was indicated. It was a sign to the world. Something clenched in his gut, but he stayed stiff and still in his seat.

"How lovely," he remarked.

Lord Barwood extended one elegant hand to Lady Katherine. She took it, rising mechanically, and the two of them took their leave, gliding out of the box with the maid in tow.

Timothy sat heavily back against his seat, watching the rapidly emptying theatre. It had seemed so magical before, but now he could see the faded velvet, the chipped gilt, the layers of dust on the mouldings and sculptures that couldn't be reached.

He spent a moment thinking of the word to describe how he felt. A true author, it didn't take him long to find it out.

Hollow. That was the world. Hollow, like a cored-out apple.

Chapter Ten

"... of course, Lord Barwood practically slept through the whole play. I could hear him yawning behind me almost incessantly," Katherine complained, pouring herself a fresh cup of tea. Fortunately, Timothy – that is, Mr. Timothy Rutherford – had a wonderful grasp of the play. We discussed it a great deal and spoke some more about the L. Sterling novels. You know, I really do think he's read them all, like he says. Not like that wretched Mr. Thompson, who claimed to have read the novels when really, he only knew the titles."

Elizabeth, who'd barely had the opportunity to say a word since Katherine had arrived, sipped her tea meditatively.

They were drinking tea in Elizabeth's private parlour, the sort of quiet conversations they often enjoyed. Elizabeth was always happy to see her friend. Katherine was such a wonderful person, and the details of her cruel father's will had upset Elizabeth far more than she cared to let on. Katherine – and her brothers – deserved so much more.

It had never bothered Elizabeth that so many people compared her unfavorably to her pretty, charming friend. It didn't much matter if gentlemen preferred Katherine to Elizabeth – Katherine herself preferred Elizabeth over any gentleman, and indeed over most people.

This business of Lord Barwood was another worrying element in a very tense storyline, in Elizabeth's opinion. She intended to write her own novels, like L. Sterling, and she was always on the lookout for new characters, new plot points, and so on.

This story was not playing out as well as she had hoped.

"You mention Timothy a great deal," she said lightly. "He seems to have been a more pleasant companion than Lord Barwood."

Katherine rolled her eyes. "I think a statue would have been a nicer companion than Lord Barwood."

"Then why," Elizabeth asked sensibly, "did you go with him?"

She flushed. "Mama thought it would be a good thing, and Will had the tickets, and *he* wanted me to go with Lord Barwood. I can't exactly go unaccompanied, any more than Amelia and Rebecca could have done. Timothy is an old friend, remember?"

"I remember," Elizabeth responded, taking a genteel sip of tea. "But if you go promenading with Lord Barwood today, you'll be seen. People will assume you're forming an understanding. Engagements happen soon after *understandings* are made public. And from what I've seen, Lord Barwood is entirely ready to offer for you, when the time is right. Have you considered what you are going to say?"

Elizabeth waited patiently for her friend to answer. She prided herself on her patience, on being able to sit still and assess a situation, to take her time in responding, to wait for others to give their answer. In Elizabeth's humble opinion – which was, in fairness, not often asked – people rushed too quickly into saying things. Words could not, after all, be taken back after being spoken.

"I will cross that bridge when I come to it," Katherine said firmly. A less than ideal answer.

Elizabeth sighed. "Oh, Kat. I wish you'd be a little more careful, that's all. I don't mean to make you feel silly, or unprepared, but it's entirely clear to me that you're not in love with Lord Barwood."

"And what does love have to do with anything?" Katherine shot back. "I don't have the leisure to think of *love* these days. My business is to make a match as soon as possible, for my family's sake. For my own sake, I hope to choose a man I like well enough to marry, but that is a secondary consideration. I haven't chosen this situation for myself, but I am in it, and there's no sense in getting upset."

She punctuated this comment with a slurp of tea. Elizabeth bit her lip, considering.

Her friend had a point. They'd talked and talked about the necessity of her marriage so many times that it seemed there was nothing more to discuss, nothing new to say. Katherine needed to marry to save her family from poverty, and that was that.

But was Lord Barwood *really* the best choice? The man was as vain as a peacock and looked straight through Elizabeth to the point of rudeness. He only seemed to notice pretty ladies, and clearly did not count Elizabeth among their ranks.

What a loss for me, she thought, smiling wryly.

"May I ask a frank question?" Elizabeth said at last.

"You always do."

"Do you have feelings for Timothy Rutherford?"

Katherine's hand jumped, slopping some tea over the side of her cup and into the saucer. Blinking at her friend, shocked, she set the cup back down with a *clack*.

"I beg your pardon?"

Elizabeth sipped her own tea. "You heard me, Kat."

More silence. Fortunately, Elizabeth was good at brazening out silence.

"Of course I don't," Katherine managed at last. "What a suggestion."

"Are you sure? You talk about him a great deal. The two of you seem to have many things in common. You clearly enjoy his company – don't pretend that you don't – and you also prefer him to Lord Barwood. Money is not an object in your marriage, so if you prefer Timothy, why not say it?"

Katherine bit her lip, looking away. "May I remind you that Timothy is one of William's oldest friends? No, he *is* my brother's oldest friend. They are very close, and I know Timothy and his family well."

"That," Elizabeth said severely, "is not what I asked."

"What I'm trying to say is that I have no doubt Timothy views me as a sister."

"Hm. And do you see him as a brother?"

It could have been the light, but Elizabeth was sure she saw a blush creep over her friend's face.

"I don't want to discuss this, Elizabeth."

"Why not?"

"Because Lord Barwood is clearly the better match. And he is the one who has shown interest in me. I'm a woman in a society that wants me to do nothing but sit and... and do needlepoint! I can't go pursuing gentlemen. If Timothy does... does have feelings for me – which he does not – he has kept them well hidden."

Elizabeth digested this information. Katherine did have a point. Timothy hadn't asked Katherine to dance, or to promenade with him, or even paid any calls on them. Nothing a gentleman might do if he had interest in a lady had been done.

"I suppose that's a point," Elizabeth admitted begrudgingly. "But if *you* like *him*, that might be a sign to put off Lord Barwood."

"I'm promenading with Lord Barwood this afternoon," Katherine said dully. "William and Mama forced me into it. I need to leave soon, to get ready. He's got a new gig he wants to show off. And I suspect he wants to show me off, too."

A prickle ran up and down Elizabeth's spine. "I don't like that man, Kat. Really, I don't."

Her friend met her gaze, and for a moment, Elizabeth thought that it was all going to come out – everything she felt, all of her worries, her feelings for Timothy, her lack of feelings for Lord Barwood.

Then Katherine's expression grew shuttered, and she looked away.

"It's not as if I'm engaged to him," she responded shortly. "I can't afford to reject every man that comes my way. Time is running out for me, Elizabeth."

That was that, then. Elizabeth had known her friend long enough to tell when a subject had been pushed far enough, and Katherine had just hit her limit. It would be wise to let the subject drop.

Perhaps Elizabeth was tired of being *wise*.

"You hate promenading," she said. "I know you do. You said it's silly, a pointless exercise designed to make statements of one sort or the other. It's just a hundred or so rich people wandering around a park, pretending to enjoy themselves and saying hello to each other. That's what you said. Your exact words."

Katherine pressed her lips together. "Perhaps so, but I also told Lord Barwood I'd go with him, and I don't intend to go back on my word."

"I thought you said William had made the promise on your behalf."

Katherine abruptly got to her feet. "Listen to me now, Elizabeth. I know you, and I love you. I know fine well you are trying to do what's best for me. I appreciate that. But the fact of the matter is that I am in a position which you can't possibly understand. There is so much pressure on my shoulders that sometimes..." she trailed off, swallowing hard. "Sometimes I feel like I can't breathe. Henry is more aloof and angrier than ever before, Alexander is sinking into a drunken depression, and William is going mad with fear and anxiety over what will happen to our family. My getting married won't solve these problems, but they will open up the way for us to get the money we desperately need. I really must be allowed to make my own decisions in this matter. I appreciate your advice, but the choices here are mine. Not yours, not William's, not Mama's. Mine."

The last word was spoken loudly and reverberated around the parlour.

Biting her lip harder this time, Elizabeth replaced her teacup and got to her feet.

"Of course," she said softly. "I'm sorry, Katherine."

Katherine relaxed a little. "You have nothing to be sorry for. I'm not... not angry at you. It's just a difficult situation."

Elizabeth nodded, pulling her friend forward into a tight hug. "I'm here for you. At least, I'll try to be."

"Thank you, Lizzie," Katherine responded, voice muffled in Elizabeth's shoulder. When they pulled apart a few moments later, Elizabeth could have sworn that her shoulder was wet with tears.

***

"Why not your red gown, Katherine?" the Duchess said for the hundredth time. "It's very becoming."

"Yes, Mama, but it's also very thin. I don't want to be cold."

The Duchess tutted. "Cold! Fancy worrying about that. Red suits you, and I'm sure Lord Barwood will admire it."

Katherine bit her lip hard, eyeing her reflection. She'd chosen a grey riding suit, which would not have been an ideal choice, but it was warm and would allow her to climb up into Lord Barwood's high gig.

He would be here at any minute.

With a dismissive gesture, the Duchess dismissed the maids, who bobbed curtsies and scuttled out.

Wonderful, Katherine thought tiredly. *A lecture.*

"My worry, Katherine," the Duchess said slowly, "is that you are not doing enough to secure the earl."

"Not doing enough? Mama, I can't throw myself at him."

The Duchess met Katherine's eyes squarely through the mirror. "You know that Lord Barwood has an interest in you. He's been very clear. This is courtship, my girl."

"I'm aware."

"If you encourage him, he'll make you an offer before the year is up. You'll be married and settled, with your own money and his into the bargain."

"Actually, that is not quite true. He will have his money, and also mine. I will be a wife."

"Don't be so silly. That's the way of the world, and you know it. Need I remind you why your marriage is so important?"

"Please do, Mama, I'd almost forgotten."

The Duchess pressed her lips together into a tight, thin line. "This sort of wit does not become you. I hope you won't treat Lord Barwood to this sort of nonsense. You must *encourage* him, Katherine. Men don't like to imagine they're dragging a girl down the aisle to the altar."

Katherine privately thought that some gentlemen would not care one way or the other, but now was naturally not the time to bring this up.

"I'll behave appropriately, Mama, I promise."

On cue, the rattle of carriage wheels on the cobblestones drifted up from outside. She moved away from the mirror and over to the window, pulling back the curtains to see.

A fine new curricle was pulling up outside, a two-horse gig with an unnervingly high perch. It was only large enough for two people, with a spot on the back where a poor chaperone would have to perch. Katherine herself would have to squeeze onto the seat beside Lord Barwood, who was currently leaping down to the pavement and smoothing out his fine waistcoat. He took a moment to admire himself in a window, patting his hair.

Katherine waited to feel something, remembering the flutter she'd felt in her chest the first moment she met him.

There was nothing. Not just the absence of emotion, but a faint flicker of disgust. Of anger. If she went downstairs now and told him how much she disliked promenading, would he agree to cancel the outing?

No, of course not.

"You can't keep him waiting," the Duchess said, sounding peevish. "Go on, go downstairs."

Katherine's legs moved her mechanically, along the hallway and down the stairs to the foyer, where a well-dressed Lord Barwood waited to greet her. He had a new coat, she noticed, with a respectably fashionable three capes, and she watched his gaze flick down her figure. Assessing, she thought, to make sure she was dressed finely and fashionably enough to be seen with him.

Apparently, her clothing met with his approval. Glancing up at her, he smiled, holding out a hand.

"Ready to go, Lady Katherine?"

Smile, she reminded herself. It was a false smile, but that didn't seem to bother him very much.

"Of course."

"It's a little chilly out there, and I intend to drive fast, so I'm glad to see you well wrapped-up. Shall we go?"

It wasn't a question, so Katherine did not respond. They went out to the curricle, and she climbed unsteadily up onto the seat. Lord Barwood sat beside her, flashed a grin, and snapped the reins. And then they were off, with nothing for her to do but keep her eyes fixed ahead and not at the ground rushing past beneath them.

He really does drive too fast, she thought sourly, as they darted past a slow-moving stagecoach, making the curricle tip worryingly to one side.

He was talking about something or other, but Katherine was not listening. Frankly, her conversation that morning with Elizabeth had left her shaken. Trust Elizabeth to say something that nobody else would.

I do not have feelings for Timothy, she told herself firmly. *He's a kind, caring gentleman, and I am glad to spend time with him. He's my brother's friend, and a good man into the bargain. I daresay he just feels sorry for me, being escorted around by Lord Barwood. No point thinking it's otherwise.*

No point getting my hopes up.

That last thought gave Katherine something of a shock. Of *course* she wasn't *hoping* that Timothy had feelings for her. And if he had, well, why would he not have said or done something to make them clear? Why shrink into the background the way he often did?

No, Timothy was nothing but a kind man. Lord Barwood was the one with an interest in Katherine.

She shot a sideways glance at the man in question, feeling a lump rising to her throat.

I don't love him, she thought wearily. *I don't know if I ever could. But time is indeed running out. Who else is there?*

Chapter Eleven

"Let me be clear, Timothy," Lord Rustford said, in a low and terrible voice, "I am not *asking* this of you. I am telling you it must be done."

Timothy clenched his jaw. The task in question was to accompany his sister, mother, and aunt to a soiree hosted by somebody or other, since Christopher and his wife had better things to do, and Lord Rustford himself was far too important to represent the family at a soiree.

"I had planned to work tonight, Father."

"Ha!" Lord Rustford gave a short laugh, shaking his head. "You'll take them, and that's final."

Of course, it was not final. Timothy could have simply laughed, turned on his heel, and walked out of his family home, picking up his coat and hat as he went.

However, it was likely he would not be permitted to return. Lord Rustford was a spiteful man, and this was not the hill Timothy was prepared to die on.

He said nothing, and this was taken as acceptance.

"Dress quickly," Lord Rustford said shortly, pushing past him to leave. "I believe your brother has some clothes you can wear. They leave at seven o' clock, sharp."

Resisting the urge to point out that the ladies would be going nowhere without their escort, Timothy gritted his teeth and followed his father.

Christopher's brown suit fitted well enough, if a little loose around the waist. Timothy tried his best to tuck in the excess fabric.

"It's sympathy weight," Christopher said defiantly, lounging in the doorway. "Constance will start to get bigger soon, and I don't want her to feel bad about herself."

"How good of you."

His brother still lingered there, and Timothy cast him a curious glance. It wasn't like Christopher, wanting to spend more time than was strictly necessary with his younger brother. Or any of his family, truthfully, with the exception of Constance.

"Is everything alright?" Timothy asked in the end. His brother glanced away.

"I shouldn't be telling you this, but I think you deserve to be told sooner rather than later."

Timothy glanced back at his reflection, heart thumping. "Oh?"

"When Constance has the baby, I intend to spend time being a father. It's an important business, having a child, and we've waited for this one for some time."

Timothy wasn't entirely sure how this affected him, but he waited patiently.

"Father intends to bring you into the business again, to take my place," Christopher said, in a rush. "Since I won't be able to work such long hours. He talked about it last night."

The hairs on the back of Timothy's neck rose. "What? I don't want to be involved with the business. I have no head for business. Besides, there's my…"

"Your what?" Christopher interrupted, sneering. "Your writing? Your *novels*? Be serious, Timothy. I'm talking about real work. You can write novels in your spare time, if you like."

Timothy opened his mouth, intending to explain just how difficult it was to write a novel, how long it took, how much it meant to him and his readers.

He closed his mouth again. There was no point. Already, Christopher was distracted, picking at his cuffs.

"Thank you," Timothy said. "Thank you for the warning."

His brother glanced sharply at him, looking a little worried now. "Warning? It's not a warning. I just thought you'd need some time to come to terms with it. You know what Father is like. This is happening, Timothy. There isn't a great deal you can do about it. Soon, it'll be all arranged, and that will be that."

"Just like how there was nothing I could do about leaving home, about choosing to be a writer, choosing to lead my own life?" Timothy shot back; voice clipped. "Just as how it was *all arranged* that I would marry Miss Somerson, the heiress, regardless of the fact I hadn't even met her, because *you* wanted to marry Constance instead. I seem to recall that despite all of those things being *all arranged*, they didn't happen."

Christopher flushed. "Be reasonable, Timothy."

"No, thank you," Timothy said coolly, affixing a cravat pin in place. It was one of Christopher's, but his brother would simply have to get over it. "I don't think I will. Do excuse me – we're leaving at seven o' clock sharp."

That wasn't the end of the conversation, of course. Christopher scurried down the stairs after him, looking nervous.

"You won't tell Father that I told you, will you? He said you weren't to know until things were in place."

"No, Christopher, of course I won't."

"Good. That's good. You know, it wouldn't be the worst thing if you were to join in the family business."

"Wouldn't? It would be the worst thing for me. I'm happy as I am, you know."

Christopher snorted. "Oh, you can't possibly be. Living in those confined apartments, no wife, not much money – it sounds dire."

"To you, I suppose, it would be."

Then they were descending the last flight of stairs, with the ladies waiting below, and Christopher was obliged to be quiet. Timothy noticed that Lord Rustford wasn't even there. Apparently, he was so certain that his orders would be carried out that he didn't bother to check whether Timothy actually arrived to escort the ladies.

You're in for a shock soon, Father, Timothy thought grimly.

Rebecca was resplendent in a pink satin gown, cut daringly low as the fashion called for these days. Amelia wore a more somber dark blue gown, flatteringly cut if not fashionably so, and Lady Rustford wore her favourite shimmering purple satin strung with pearls.

"There you are, Timothy," she snapped. "It's a lady's prerogative to be late, not a gentleman's."

Timothy glanced at the clock, which read five minutes to seven. "I don't believe I am late, Mother."

She didn't bother to respond, choosing instead to go sailing outside to where the carriage awaited. Rebecca hurried after her, but Amelia paused to slip her arm through Timothy's.

"It'll be alright, Timmy," she said quietly. "Come along, let's go."

The soiree – held at Lady Georgiana Black's home – was a fabulous event indeed. The heat and noise hit Timothy as soon as he stepped through the door, making his skin prickle under his borrowed clothing. It was clear at once that this was going to be a *crush* of an evening.

Lady Rustford disappeared at once, and Rebecca was swallowed up by a crowd of friends, leaving Amelia and Timothy alone.

"I hate these affairs," Amelia sighed. "I can't go around with the young people, on account of being a *spinster*, and the matrons don't want me to sit with them, because I'm not married."

"Then why do you go?"

She shot him a look. "Because my sister and my brother-in-law have decided that I must. I live on their generosity, Timmy."

"Well, if I marry a rich woman, you can come and live with us."

She chuckled. "I'm sure that your beautiful, rich heiress will not want your old aunt living with you."

"She won't just be beautiful and rich. She'll be kind, too. And she'll love you."

"You're a sweet boy, Timmy."

"I'm a man, Aunt. And please, don't call me Timmy here. I'm not sure I'd live it down. In fact, if we're overheard..."

He trailed off when a familiar face and figure glided across the room, just ahead. Space was clearing in the middle of the ballroom in preparation for the first dance of the evening, and he clearly saw Katherine step across it, beside one of her brothers.

She was breathtakingly beautiful, so beautiful Timothy could not quite understand how others were going about their business, barely glancing at her. The whole room should have gone silent. Everyone should have been looking at her, awestruck.

Instead, the noise and chaos filled the room, as always, and nobody really looked at her.

Lady Katherine Willoughby was wearing a forest-green gown, the skirt flimsy and gauzy, the bodice tight and the neckline almost as daringly low as Rebecca's. A myriad of embroidered silk flowers clustered around the neckline and waistline, and trailing vines and flowers curled down the skirts of the dress, almost like real plants.

And then she turned and saw him, and her face lit up.

Timothy was entirely sure that his heart had stopped. He sucked in a breath, suddenly realized that he had been holding it. Katherine said something to her brother – it was Alexander, Timothy could see now – and began to glide towards them.

He opened his mouth, intending to tell Amelia that Katherine was here and coming to speak with them, but when he glanced down at his aunt, she was already looking at him, a curious, thoughtful expression on her face.

There was no time to say anything, because then Katherine was there.

"Lady Amelia, Timothy, how good to see you!" she said, smiling. "It's so busy here tonight. I've already been elbowed in the ribs twice, and I think somebody stood on the hem of my dress."

"Oh, dear," Amelia sighed. "And it's such a pretty dress, too. I never had chance to ask you, did you enjoy the play last night? Lord Barwood rushed you out so quickly."

If Timothy hadn't known better, he might have thought that Katherine rolled her eyes. Then the moment was gone, and she was smiling easily at them.

"Oh, I certainly did. Although Timothy and I *did* talk a good deal through it. We were talking about my favourite subject – L. Sterling novels. He's quite knowledgeable."

Amelia smiled at him. "Yes, my nephew is very knowledgeable when it comes to novels."

"Does anyone else have any theories about when the final installment of *Rosalie's Trials* will be released? I'm on tenterhooks, and nobody seems to know. It's a guarded secret, it seems."

Timothy grimaced, taking a sip of his champagne. "It has to be finished within two months, or else."

There was a brief silence.

"You seem very sure," Katherine said, tilting her head. "How do you know that?"

He froze.

Idiot. You've got to think before you speak?

"Oh, I just... just assumed, I suppose. I don't know any more than anyone else. I'm just *assuming* that it will be released soon. The author – whoever he is – will be under a great deal of pressure to finish it. Or she, naturally. Nobody knows who L. Sterling is, after all."

He was babbling, gabbling on and on about nonsense, and Katherine's eyebrows were creeping up towards her hairline. Amelia quietly pinched his arm, and Timothy took the hint to be quiet.

"Well," Katherine said, after an awkward pause, "I came here to bring you my favourite novel. You said you've read them all, but this one is *so* obscure I'm sure you mustn't have read it."

Glancing furtively around, she reached into a pocket in her skirts – an excellent invention, in Timothy's opinion – and drew out a small, blue-covered volume. It was well-read, tattered and yellowed, with the bindings faded and the spine long since broken.

He knew the title of the book long before he read it etched into the title page.

"*Jeremiah's Heart*," he read aloud. "*By L. Sterling.* This... this is the first Sterling novel. Hardly anyone bought it."

"I bought it," Katherine laughed. "And I loved it. It's fitting that the author's first novel should inspire me to read all the rest of his books. I want you to read it, then we can talk about it."

Timothy swallowed hard, clutching the book until his eyes blurred. He remembered writing this novel, scribbling when he could, still living at home, his dreams of being a novelist seeming further and further away with each passing day. He remembered

Christopher, in a fit of pique, tossing his half-finished manuscript into the fire and claiming it was an accident. He remembered writing the story again from scratch.

"Will you read it?" Katherine said, sounding anxious. He glanced up to find her looking up at him hopefully.

"Yes," he said, voice a little thick. "I'll read it very carefully and give you my honest opinion."

She beamed, clearly thrilled to have found a novel which he had not yet read. Before they could exchange another word, Amelia cleared her throat somewhat pointedly.

"I see that Lord Barwood is heading our way," she said calmly.

Timothy's heart, already fluttering hard, sunk into his stomach like a stone.

Just perfect.

Did he see a flash of disappointment on Katherine's face, too? Whatever it was, it disappeared quickly, and then the man himself arrived.

"Good evening, ladies, gentleman," Lord Barwood said, grinning. "What a surprise to see you out, Timothy. You usually seem to prefer the quiet of your dull little apartment."

Timothy considered pointing out what a rude thing that was to say but decided against it. He would swallow his annoyance, once again.

Lord Barwood evidently did not intend to stay for much conversation. He turned on his heel, offering his arm to Katherine with a smile.

"The first dance is beginning; shall we take our places?"

She took it, smiling tightly. Lord Barwood glanced over at Arthur, smile widening.

"I hope to convince Lady Katherine to dance with me twice tonight. I'm not sure I can allow her to dance with any other gentlemen."

He laughed, as if the comment was a joke. Nobody else laughed. And then they were gone, sweeping across the dance floor, quickly getting lost in the crowd.

"I do not like that man," Amelia muttered.

Timothy let out a sigh, feeling deflated. At least she'd had the chance to leave the book with him. He had no doubt that Lord Barwood would keep all other gentlemen – himself included – away from her for the rest of the night. He turned to walk away, but found himself tugged back, hauled face to face with his aunt.

"What exactly do you think you are doing, Timothy?" she demanded.

He blinked. "I... I was going to find some refreshments."

"And leave poor Katherine with that wretch? Did she *look* happy to be cornered by him for the rest of the evening?"

"No, but..." Timothy floundered. "What am I to do?"

"Do? *Do*? Timothy, I have watched you with that woman for quite some time now. I would bet my entire fortune – not that I have much – that you are in love with her."

He flinched. "Aunt, please, don't be so loud."

"Are you afraid? Afraid of her finding out? Afraid of others, of that awful Lord Barwood?"

"No, no, I just..." he looked around, trying to collect his thoughts. "She is kind to me, and friendly, but it would be wrong of me to assume she has feelings for me. I've known her since we were young. I'm friends with William, after all."

"That means nothing. Nothing. If you told her how you feel and she rejected you, that would be one thing, but I know quite well that is not what has happened. You, Timothy, are choosing the easy option."

"I don't think that's fair, Aunt."

Amelia took a step closer, eyes intent on his face. "I think that years of dealing with your parents have left you rather passive. Nobody will hand you things in life, Timothy. You must work for them. You must fight for them. Isn't that woman worth fighting for? Isn't she worth risking a little embarrassment more?"

The answer, popping into Timothy's head from nowhere, was a resounding *yes*.

"I don't know what to do," he murmured. The music had begun, and the dancing started.

"You can begin by asking her to dance," Amelia said firmly. "Once this first set is over. Get past Lord Barwood and *ask* her. Now go, my boy. Go!"

Chapter Twelve

If the rest of the night was going to pass like this, Katherine was going to die of boredom.

She'd danced with Lord Barwood, and of course couldn't dance with him again so soon. She'd assumed that he would be obliged to leave her alone in the meantime, but she was heartily wrong about that.

Hustling her away from the dance floor as soon as the set was concluded, he'd gotten her a seat in the corner, and stood over her like a jailer.

A few other gentlemen eyed her, half-determined to go over and ask her to dance, but a steely glare from Lord Barwood warned them off. A few of her friends made as if to come and join her, but Lord Barwood and the Duchess — who'd settled herself behind Katherine immediately, as if it were all planned — would instantly begin talking, turning their backs, and making it clear that the friends were not wanted here.

Elizabeth, of course, would never have fallen for such weak tricks, but Elizabeth was nowhere to be seen. Politeness did not allow Katherine to get up and stride away, and so she was trapped.

"I wonder, Lord Barwood," Katherine said, desperately, "could you fetch me some lemonade?"

Once he was gone, she could make her excuses and scurry away, in pretense of finding him, then disappear into the crowd.

"You don't need any more lemonade, Katherine," the Duchess responded crisply, and that was that. "Why don't you tell Lord Barwood about that delightful sampler you finished today?"

Katherine's heart sank. So this was it, then? She was going to spend the entire ball talking about samplers and water colours, while Lord Barwood chuckled at the vanity of women and the pointlessness of their activities?

It wasn't even a very good sampler.

"Oh, Mama, I..." she trailed off, seeing a familiar figure elbow his way through the crowd.

It was Timothy, and he looked determined. A wave of affection swept over Katherine, more powerful than she might have expected.

Lord Barwood followed her gaze, and his expression dropped sourly.

"Mr. Timothy Rutherford," he said lightly. "How unexpected."

"How pleasant to see you, Timothy," the Duchess said, her tone indicating that it was anything but. "I believe Katherine was just saying how much she would like some lemonade."

He smiled tightly. "I'm afraid I didn't come over here to fetch lemonade, your Grace. I came to see if Lady Katherine would like to dance."

Lord Barwood was glaring at Timothy as if he hoped to bore a hole through his head with his gaze. Timothy smiled easily back, meeting his gaze unflinchingly.

"Are you sure that's a good idea, Timothy?" Lord Barwood said easily. "I seem to recall you have two left feet. We wouldn't want our dear Lady Katherine to be embarrassed, would we?"

Timothy's gaze slipped past Lord Barwood, landing on Katherine. When their eyes met, a strange frisson ran through her. It was an odd feeling, something she hadn't experienced before.

Might be a chill. Or maybe I'm just extremely tired.

"I'll try my best to live up to Lady Katherine's high standards," he said lightly.

Katherine got to her feet, shaking out her skirts. "I should love to dance, Timothy. Lead the way."

He smiled, holding out his hand. She took it.

"It's not like you to stand up to Lord Barwood," Katherine commented, letting Timothy lead the way through the crowd.

"I am aware I'm usually quite a coward," he said over his shoulder, smiling tightly.

"Coward is not the word I'd use. I would have said reserved, or perhaps even a peacemaker. You don't care to use sharp words and confrontations, and that is not something to hold against you," she responded. Was it her imagination, or did his fingers tighten around hers, just a little?

"You're very kind. I thought you needed rescuing."

"You're right," she chuckled. "Lord Barwood and my dear mother seemed intent on cornering me all night. If you could keep me away from them, I'd appreciate it."

"Your mother seems to approve of Lord Barwood as a suitor for you."

She glanced sharply up at him, and Timothy bit his lip, looking away. It was too personal a question, and they both knew it.

But then, don't I know him as well as I know my brothers?

"She does," Katherine responded at last. "I can't blame her, I suppose. All she wants is for us to all be respectable and happy. I could do worse than an earl."

Timothy was quiet for a long moment after that. They took their places on the dance floor, the air shimmering with anticipation. It was going to be a waltz, Katherine realized with a flutter of excitement. The waltz was still causing a stir in the polite world, after all.

Would I have agreed to the dance if I had known? She wondered briefly. The answer came almost at once.

Yes.

The music began, and the partners bowed and curtsied to each other. Katherine and Timothy moved towards each other, neither of them speaking. The position was closer than she was comfortable with, her chin almost brushing his shoulder, their fingers interlaced, his hand resting on her waist, hers on his shoulder.

When did Timothy get this tall? She wondered, suppressing a smile. *It seems like only yesterday William and he were so small. But then, of course, I was small, too.*

"I have yet to become proficient in the art of the waltz," Timothy said, breaking the silence.

"Me neither. Still, one must move with the times, yes? Fashion and time wait for no one."

"Is that a quote?" she said, laughing. "From *Key to Emmeline Manor*? The L. Sterling novel?"

"Yes, it is. I should really quote from different novels, shouldn't I? You'll think that's all I read."

"There are worse things to read than novels. L. Sterling novels, at all."

The dance required them to move apart, Katherine twirling under Timothy's arm.

"We danced like this – not the waltz, naturally – when we were children, do you remember?" she said, and a smile spread across his face.

"Yes, yes, I recall. I tripped over my own feet and trod on your hem at least once."

"More than once, I should say. My poor feet – you stood on them so many times."

The dance slowed again, and this time, the talk flowed easily. The waltz, for all its controversies, allowed plenty of time and breath for talk. Katherine could not even recall what they talked about, just that she was laughing and so was he, and she kept catching glimpses of faces in the crowds, blurs that didn't matter because the dance and the man who held her close were all that mattered.

When the music stopped, it was almost a jarring sensation. The partners separated, laughing, clapping, bowing to each other, and Katherine was obliged to follow suit. She caught a glimpse of Lord Barwood in the crowd, arms folded tight, not smiling. He made as if to move forward, to claim her again, but she turned her back, and he had the grace to stop.

"Thank you," she said, when the commotion died down somewhat, and the dancers were clearing the floor to make room for the next sets of partners. "For asking me to dance."

Timothy smiled, and she could have sworn she saw a flush rise to his cheeks. But then, perhaps it was the heat of the room.

"No need to thank me. I should be thanking you, for being patient with me. I should have asked you to dance a long time ago."

"We already did dance, remember? A long time ago, as we said."

He smiled again, distantly this time. "It was different. Much different."

A tingle ran down her spine, something unfamiliar and not entirely unpleasant.

She spotted Elizabeth up ahead, coming through the crowd, smiling. She wouldn't have to sit with Lord Barwood and her mother any more tonight. She was free.

Timothy was already melting away, disappearing into the crowd. Katherine did not want him to go, and that realization hit her like a four-horse chaise.

Stop, whispered a small, intent voice in the back of her head. *What are you doing? What are you thinking? He's an old friend, a friend of your brother's. He was being kind, that's all. You have no right to feel this way about him.*

But that didn't help. If anything, it drew her attention to the feelings that were already there, the ones she didn't dare investigate. The ones that made her chest tighten and a lump rise to her throat.

"Thank you, Timothy," she said, although she wasn't entirely sure he heard before he disappeared into the crowd.

Chapter Thirteen

To Mr. Rutherford, Referencing our Previous Conversation
I hope you and your family are in good health. I am writing to remind you of the upcoming deadline, and to ask if there is any progress in the third Rosalie volume. I read in the scandal sheets that you have been attending various balls and events with your family, and while your socialising is to be congratulated, I feel it my duty to remind you of yours.

The world is waiting for the final instalment of Rosalie's adventures, Timothy. I would take it as a personal favour if you would concentrate on writing as much as you can, before the approach of the deadline. The earlier, the better.

Thank you.
Your Colleague, Mr. Hawthorne

The letter, slightly crumpled and shoved aside, rolled onto the floor from the desk when Timothy pushed the half-finished manuscript aside.

Half finished. He was so close to the end of Rosalie's adventures.

The past few days had been full of a flurry of writing, and most recently of all, Timothy had stayed up all night to finish a particularly tense section, before he lost his inspiration. The sun was up now, and he hadn't slept a wink.

I don't even feel tired, he thought, smiling wryly. No sooner had the thought left his head when a knock came on the door.

Well, it can't be my landlady – my rent is all paid up.

Opening the door, Timothy was surprised to find Amelia and Rebecca standing on the doorstep.

"Rebecca and I have just subscribed to the new Library," Amelia said, before he could get in a word. "You ought to subscribe, too. I'm sure they'll have those novels you were talking about."

"I... I am working."

"You are always working," Rebecca huffed, unceremoniously elbowing past her brother and stepping inside. "You know how father disapproves of circulating libraries, and novels in general. He wasn't going to let us go. Not unless you escorted us."

Timothy caught Amelia's eye at that, and she hastily looked away.

There were not many places that a respectable lady could go, but a library was one of them. The larger, more serious libraries boasted mostly theological and scientific works, which of course ladies of note did not bother their heads to read, even if they were admitted in the door.

The circulating libraries were different. Timothy had watched their popularity grow over the years, their stores of books ranging from novels – Mrs. Radcliff and Mrs. Burney being intensely popular – to history, science, travel, poetry, and so on. They were, in his opinion, a very good thing indeed.

He could imagine how frustrated it would make Amelia and Rebecca feel, knowing that Lord Rustford had the power to cut them off from this enjoyment altogether.

"Very well," he said at last. "I'll come with you."

***

The new Library was run by a woman named Mrs. Steele, a serious-faced widow who eyed Timothy with great suspicion. Some of her wariness dissipated when she realised that he was here to escort his sister and aunt, her patrons, and intended to subscribe himself.

"We have a great many books here, sir," she said quickly, once she began to see that he was going to be a patron. "Many learned books, from authors of note. Some persons seem to think that circulating libraries like this are all novels, but I can assure you..."

"No need to cater to my pride, Mrs. Steele," he interrupted with a smile. "I'm very fond of novels. Extremely fond, in fact."

The woman visibly relaxed. "Ah, I'm glad. I try to keep something of everything here, regardless of prejudice. We even have one or two copies of *Fordyce's* works; can you believe it?"

"The same book in which he condemned novels?" Timothy said, laughing. "That is surprising. I admire your kindness."

She leaned towards him conspiratorially. "We keep Fordyce next to Miss Austen and Mrs. Radcliffe."

He suppressed a snort. "Very good, Mrs. Steele, very good."

The Library itself was a large one, set in a good-sized room. There was plenty of seating available, along with refreshments and tea to buy. About a dozen ladies of varying ages browsed the bookshelves, and one well-groomed gentleman who seemed to be something of a dandy. Timothy saw that his sister and aunt had retired to a long window seat, and were already reading, leaving Timothy to his own devices.

Smiling to himself, he began to browse the shelves.

As Mrs. Steele had said, there was a great variety of books, with regular gaps showing where the books had been borrowed out. Some books were almost new, others worn almost to shreds, but they all bore the distinctive marbled flyleaf inside the covers.

He took out a copy of *Pamela,* which was all the rage at the moment – tea sets could be bought with the heroine's likeness on it – and began to flip through the pages.

"A rather cheap choice, even for a famous novel-reader," remarked a familiar voice. Heat swept through Timothy's face, and he couldn't quite keep a wide smile from his lips.

She's here.

"Lady Katherine," he said aloud. "I can't say I'm surprised to see you here. You patronise most of the circulating Libraries at the moment, if my sister is to be believed."

Lady Katherine was leaning against a shelf, a small volume of a book half-concealed in her hands. She grinned wickedly, and Timothy could have sworn his heart skipped a beat.

"Indeed, I do. I must say, I'm surprised to see you with *Pamela*."

He glanced down at it. "Well, it's a rather famous work. As it is currently in vogue for the heroines of novels to make allusions to other esteemed literary works, I thought I'd better...better give it a read."

Better use it in Rosalie's final volume, he'd almost said, but caught himself just in time.

Lady Katherine didn't seem to have noticed his *faux pas*. Instead, she wrinkled her nose at the novel.

"Have you read it?"

"No, but I'm familiar with the story."

"No novel has ever infuriated me like that one. The character herself – poor, sweet Pamela, little more than a child – was nice enough, but the hero and villain, all rolled into one..." she shuddered. "Ugh."

He winced, glancing back down at the novel.

The story of Pamela had been all anyone could talk about. The story starts with a young – very young – and beautiful young woman, Pamela, working as a maid in a wealthy and dissolute man's house, after the death of his mother, her employer. The man took a liking to Pamela, but what started as a sweet, awkward romance quickly spiraled into something terrible.

Refusing to become the man's mistress, Pamela tries to protect her virtue as strongly as the so-called hero tries to take it. He tries to trick her, imprison her, and even assault her, and only luck and well-timed swoons saved her, time and again.

"It was difficult to read," Lady Katherine stated, after a while. "When I first read it, I expected Pamela to make her escape and return home, or else find a savior somewhere else. Imagine my shock when she reveals she'd loved him all this time, and agrees to become his wife."

"Spoilers," he remarked dryly.

"Oh, come, I simply don't want you to be blindsided. And then their engagement – oh, I don't want to talk about it. I was never so angry at a novel in my life. I threw it across the room. And then, all my friends were talking about how romantic it was, how virtuous she was, and so on. As if marrying that brute was meant to be her reward."

"I suspect it was."

"Are you *sure* you want to read Pamela? I have a few more novels to recommend, if you would appreciate a heroine with a more spirited demeanour."

"I think it has to be this one," Timothy responded sadly. This was the novel pointed out to him by his publisher, and Mr. Hawthorne was already running out of patience with him. "What book do you have there?"

Lady Katherine hesitated, just for a moment, then showed him.

Timothy flinched. The book was a small, red-bound volume, with a familiar title on the front, a single name.

"*Thomasin*," he read aloud. "That's one of L. Sterling's earliest works. Very unpopular, I recall."

"Not unpopular, just little-known. It's a quiet sort of book, without the terrifying scenes and villains of the later books."

"Do... do you prefer those scenes to the quiet ones?"

She chuckled. "That depends entirely what mood I'm in. This is one thing I love about the author – they can write soft, gentle stories, and nerve-wracking tense ones, but their style and integrity never falters. That's a rare thing to find in an author these days. Even Shakespeare wrote the kind of plays audiences wanted to see, and one has to wonder how much of his artistic integrity was sacrificed to that."

"Goodness, you seem to understand these matters very well," Timothy laughed, thinking of his editor and endless, loud meetings in which he was begged to alter his stories to appeal more to 'audiences', although these audiences were never exactly identified.

"And what is that supposed to mean?" she retorted, laughing.

"It means that you ought to write stories of your own, Lady Katherine. Have you ever thought of becoming an author?"

She shrugged, flicking through the pages of *Thomasin*. "I'm sure I wouldn't know where to start."

"Nonsense. Somebody who reads as much as you do would write a remarkable story, I'm sure of it."

"I'm glad *you're* sure of it. You know how publishers baulk at a woman writing fiction. Or non-fiction, for that matter."

Or a man writing novels.

"Use a pseudonym," he suggested. "Most famous authors do."

"Like this one?" Lady Katherine said, holding up *Thomasin*. "Everybody knows that L. Sterling is a pseudonym. We're split between thinking that the author is female and male."

"And which do you believe?"

"I think the author is female. Or perhaps I'd simply like to believe that. And you?"

"Male, I think. But of course, I don't know anything about it."

"Did you ever meet an author you admired?" Katherine asked, turning to the moth-eaten flyleaf.

A prickle ran down his spine. "No, I don't believe so. Why? Have you?"

"No, but I'd very much like to meet L. Sterling. I know it's foolish to fixate so much on one author – there are so many accomplished and talented writers now, after all – but I always felt like Sterling could see into a reader's head. The characters leap over the page. I don't mind saying that I've cried at the ending of more than one of his books. This one, for starters."

She held up *Thomasin*. Timothy swallowed, hard.

He recalled the ending. Thomasin, having endured many trials and saved her younger sisters from a fever, succumbs to the fever herself. Her death is peaceful, and a good end to the story, but readers did not like it. They felt as though the story was unfinished, somehow.

"Thomasin never gets her revenge," he said, half to himself. "Her betrothed jilts her and passes out of the story – he's never punished. In the end, it hints that her father gives up drink to care for his family better, but are we sure that happens? Did Thomasin really make any progress in her life at all, or was her death entirely in vain? It's disappointing, I think."

Katherine eyed him for a long moment, and Timothy felt heat rising to his cheeks.

"It's a first novel," she said at last. "It's not perfect. But it is interesting. The author hadn't quite established their style, hadn't quite found their feet in the world of writing. This is, I think, one of the most raw and honest novels I have ever read. You can feel the author's pain – their fear about irrelevance, about living in vain, about never quite making the changes they long to see. About being alone. That was what Thomasin feared most, wasn't it? Being alone. The author is living through their character, to an extent that I would say they aren't even separate entities anymore."

There was a long, taut pause after that. Katherine flushed, looking away.

"Silly, I know."

"It's not silly," Timothy said at once. He was breathless. Why was he breathless? "That's a very insightful remark."

"Well, I'm sure if I met the author, they would tell me it's nonsense, and I don't know what I'm talking about."

Timothy swallowed hard. "I don't believe they would say that at all."

She smiled wryly. "Hm. Well, I must go – I think Elizabeth is waiting for me, we're having tea here before we leave. But I'll see you at the masquerade tomorrow night, yes?"

"Yes, I think so."

"What are you dressing up as?"

He swallowed again. "Honestly, I have no idea."

Chapter Fourteen

The masquerade was to be held at the Argyle Rooms. Katherine had never been there before. The queue to get in the door trailed down the steps up to the main entrance, which did not bode well for the state of affairs inside. Katherine was shivering in the night air, but suspected she would warm up all too quickly once she was inside.

"Ridiculous waste of time," Henry was muttering, chafing in his outfit. Alexander and he were black and white dominos respectively, with long, flowing cloaks, tight suits, and knee-high boots. William had decided not to wear a mask and could have been going to any party in London, albeit with a long, patchwork cloak which he'd been pressured into throwing on at the last minute. The Duchess had also elected not to dress up, donning a light, lacy black mask as a concession. She had her lips pressed together, and did not appear particularly happy.

"Oh, try and relax a little, Henry," Alexander chuckled. His eyes were bright, and Katherine suspected he'd already been drinking brandy before they left home. William seemed to be distracted, and Henry was eyeing his younger brother sharply, obviously suspecting the same as Katherine.

"What are you going as again, Kat?" Alexander continued, a little too jovially. She could smell the brandy on his breath now and exchanged a quick look with Henry.

"I'm Athena, Alexander. You know, the Greek goddess?"

"I know who Athena is," Alexander mumbled. "A little too high brow for a *masquerade*, though. I hear that Miss Bragg is going as a marionette's doll. That'll be interesting, I'm sure."

"Oh, yes," Katherine retorted acidly.

In truth, she wasn't entirely sure whether Athena was the right guise for her. In keeping with the Grecian style, she was wearing a long, white robe, made of shifts and veils all draped together and pinned in various places, hanging down to her sandaled feet. Her arms were bare, and the costume was fixed in place with brooches on the top of each shoulder. It was looser than she was used to and felt somewhat flimsy. She'd done her hair in a simple Grecian style, twisted back at the nape of her neck, and had a head-dress on top, and a simple gold-coloured mask.

The effect had been very nice in the mirror in her bedroom, but now Katherine was a little worried that someone might tread on her hem and tear the whole costume away.

And then they were inside the marbled halls, and as expected, the heat and noise hit them like a wave.

One by one, her family disappeared. William trailed off, Alexander made a beeline for the refreshments and glasses of champagne, and Henry followed him, looking grim.

That left Katherine and her mother. The Duchess looped her arm firmly through her daughter's, and Katherine realised with a sinking heart that she wasn't going to get away anytime soon.

"Shall we look out Lord Barwood?" the Duchess said lightly. "I wonder what he is dressed as tonight. Something sensible, I'm sure."

"I'd... I'd rather not, Mama. Lord Barwood tends to monopolise me. I'd like to spend time with my friends, and mingling. He practically keeps me prisoner when we're not dancing."

The Duchess pressed her lips together. "Lord Barwood is simply staking his claim."

"Staking his *claim*? I am not something to be claimed, Mama."

"Don't be silly. I suppose we have all that novel-reading nonsense to thank for this attitude. Lord Barwood is an eminently suitable gentleman, and one you should be proud to make a match with. Besides, I don't need to remind you that he is the only gentleman who has expressed interest in you so far."

Yes, because he's scaring off everyone else, Katherine thought sourly. Even then, though, there was an element of doubt.

Timothy came to mind again, no matter how hard she tried not to. Their conversation the other day, in between the bookshelves of the circulating Library, had rung in her head over and over again. At first, she'd worried that she had seemed silly, or overly sentimental, talking about *Thomasin* the way she had. But then she had met Timothy's eye and seen something there, something... something elusive eluded her grasp.

She swallowed hard. *Stop it, Katherine. You know he only feels like a brother towards you. No point in thinking otherwise. You'll only... only set yourself up for disappointment.*

On cue, a gentleman in a red domino came lurching towards her, grinning. His uneven, yellowing teeth marked him out as one Mr. Burles, oldest son of a wealthy merchant.

"Lady Katherine!" he burbled, making a low and wobbly bow. "Can I tempt you to dance with me? I believe the dancing is just starting up."

She swallowed hard. "I... I would love to, Mr. Burles."

There was not, of course, any other answer she could make.

Within the first few minutes of the dance, it became embarrassingly clear that Mr. Burles was too drunk to be dancing. He stumbled, trod on her toes – which hurt, since she was only wearing sandals – and consistently missed steps, even going the wrong way in a promenade, which would have caused chaos if Katherine hadn't yanked him back the right way.

"Oh, dear," he said, giggling, clearly too drunk even to comprehend how much of a fool he was being. "Thank heavens you are here, eh?"

She smiled uncomfortably, trying to avoid supporting his weight. Of course, if one's dance partner was a fool, one would end up looking a fool, too. It was terribly unfair. Ladies could not refuse an invitation to dance, but a poor dancer would reflect badly on them.

Thankfully, the first dance was not a lengthy one. The music ended, and Katherine curtsied to her partner with immeasurable relief. She turned, looking for some acquaintance to hail, but wasn't quite quick enough.

"Let's have a glass of champagne each, eh?" Mr. Burles muttered in her ear, his breath sour. "And we'll find a quiet corner to talk. You know, I scarcely have had the opportunity to speak to you this Season, what with Lord Barwood keeping you all to himself. Is there an understanding between you, or what?"

"I hardly think this is a fit subject for a party, Mr. Burles," Katherine said sharply, intending to nip the conversation in the bud, and hopefully shame him into leaving her alone.

It did not work. Mr. Burles only chuckled, mumbling something about 'an admirable spirit', and steered her roughly towards the refreshment table. Katherine was just thinking about the best way to escape when a masked gentleman stepped in front of them.

He didn't speak. The gentleman was dressed as Apollo, Katherine realised after a pause. He wore loose robes that fell to mid-thigh, gathered in at the waist with a leather belt, and rough, tight breeches underneath for modesty. His hair hung in loose curls, and most of his face, from forehead almost to his lips, was covered by a plain mask. Mr. Burles moved to step around him, pulling Katherine behind him, but the man moved in front of him, hand out to stop him.

"What, what?" Mr. Burles snapped, annoyed. "What do you want? Move aside, we're going for champagne. Why don't you speak?"

Apollo shook his head dolefully and stretched out a hand towards Katherine. A warmth spread through her chest. He seemed familiar, but with the strange robes and mask, she could not tell who it was.

"I believe our Apollo is asking me to dance," Katherine said, with a half-smile. She received a bow in response. "I accept."

"But we were going to talk," Mr. Burles said unhappily.

Katherine ignored him, taking Apollo's hand. He led her off to the dance floor, where pairs of people were already lined up, in expectation of the dance.

It was a slow dance this time, a stately measure. Most of the other dancers had chosen courtesan outfits, fashionable dresses, things with colour and swathes of material, so the two masked Grecian deities earned a couple of strange stares.

Katherine found that for the first time, she did not care. She and her Apollo bowed to each other, and the dance began.

"You're not speaking," she said, thoughtfully.

A shake of the head.

"Ah. That must mean that I know you, and I would recognise your voice if you spoke. That also explains that larger mask."

Apollo's lips, the only part of him revealed by the mask, curved into a smile. The familiar feeling of *knowing* shivered through Katherine again. She longed to step forward and yank off the mask.

That, of course, would not be appropriate in the slightest.

"It's right that you're Apollo, by the way," she remarked, after a moment or two. "Apollo was always a savior, somebody who protected those who could not protect myself. The way you swept in and saved me from Mr. Burles was extremely heroic."

Again, came the smile. The dance called for the partners to spin away from each other, turning their backs for a minute. She heard him speak, his voice low and gruff, as if trying to disguise it.

"I believe you could have saved yourself."

She smiled. When they faced each other again, Apollo's face was smooth and serious, with no sign that he'd ever talked at all.

"Come, tell me who you are," Katherine said. A shake of the head was her only response. "Ah, do you intend to melt away once the dance is finished? Nod for yes, shake your head for no, and shrug your shoulders if you are undecided."

Apollo shrugged his shoulders. He was smiling now, lips twisting in a lopsided grin that seemed so familiar to Katherine that she wanted to scream in frustration.

She was feeling a little something of everything, it seemed. Her heart pounded, butterflies fluttered wildly in her stomach, and something *burned* inside her, something she hadn't quite experienced before. Apollo seemed so familiar and yet so strange, but she couldn't recall ever feeling quite so attracted to a man in her life.

He was watching her intently, eyes shadowed by the mask, but she could still see them. He watched her hungrily but deferentially, never touching her or stepping too close except when the dance required it.

"Do you read, Apollo?"

A nod.

"Do you read novels, or do you turn up your nose at them?"

There was a muffled burst of laughter, which Apollo turned his head to hide. He nodded, and she lifted her eyebrows.

"Which is it, then? You read them, or you despise them?"

He held up one finger. Katherine found that she was enjoying their strange method of communication. It was something different, and a far cry from the stiff, soulless conversation topics usually favoured at parties.

"So you read them. How exciting – I do like a man to read novels. I find that people who despise novels are either terrible bores or simply haven't read them. Or, there is another possibility – they read novels and love them, but their pride does not allow them to admit it. I find that men are the most common culprits here."

A smile, and a nod.

"Have you read *Pamela,* Apollo?"

There was a brief hesitation, then he nodded.

"What did you think? Did you like it?"

A shake of the head.

"Ah, good. Poor Pamela did not have a happy ending, in my humble opinion. But, of course, one should not discuss novels at a masquerade – one should exchange gossip, flutter at handsome, eligible ladies and gentlemen, and try and guess who is who underneath the masks and costumes. I'm usually quite good at this, but you are proving quite a challenge, Apollo. Quite a challenge indeed."

On that note, the music ended with a flourish, and the partners drew away from each other, bowing and curtseying. Katherine clapped, eyes on her Apollo. He made no move to melt away into the crowd. She was determined, now, to find out who he was. She knew him, she was sure of it. If he would only *speak*.

"Since you cannot speak," she said thoughtfully, "I suppose I must suggest refreshments, then?"

He nodded and offered his arm. Katherine took it, and they weaved their way through the crowd. When her hand touched his bare forearm, a sensation of tingling spread across her skin, causing the fine hairs on her arm to stand on end. It was so shocking and immediate a reaction that she sucked in a sharp breath, earning herself a questioning look from Apollo.

"I'm quite alright," she managed, smiling up at him. "I just... just found myself in something of a draft."

He lifted his eyebrows at that, and rightly so. A draft in the heated ballroom seemed almost ridiculous.

"What do you think of L. Sterling, Apollo? Or Mrs. Radcliffe, or Frances Burney? Have you a favourite novelist?"

A shake of the head, a pause, then he held up two fingers.

She lifted her eyebrows. "The second author? Mrs. Radcliffe? Ah, yes, a good choice. Her *Mysteries of Udolpho* kept me breathless until the last page. *The Italian* was even better."

He nodded, smiling at her, and Katherine felt that warmth again, spreading through her chest as if she were sinking into a deep bath of hot water.

"L. Sterling is my favourite," she continued, for all the world as if she were not holding up two sides of the conversation. "I'm not entirely sure which of their books I like the best. I think... I think perhaps the most recent one, *Rosalie's Trials*."

This was not entirely true, but Katherine often grew tired of explaining her real favourite, *Jeremiah's Heart*. After all, that was not a household name, and the plot was so tragic that she had often seen eyebrows lift when she explained it.

Apollo paused, glancing down at her. If it hadn't been for the mask, she would have thought he was frowning.

"I thought *Jeremiah's Heart* was your favourite, Katherine."

Goosebumps broke out all over Katherine's body. That voice – of course she knew him. It seemed ridiculous now, thoroughly ridiculous, that she'd been standing by this man for so long and had not known him. Wasn't that his hair, curling above the mask, his lips twisting into that lopsided grin? Shouldn't she have known him from the second he stepped in front of her and Mr. Burles?

Apollo's eyes widened behind the mask, obviously knowing that he had betrayed himself. He dropped his arm, and she could have sworn that he was blushing. He did blush, though, she remembered that much. No cool and collected gentleman was this, and Katherine knew without a drop of uncertainty that she wouldn't want him any other way.

"Thank you for dancing with me," he mumbled, the confident masked Apollo gone at once. "I am sorry to take up so much of your time. I... I'll go. I should have just told you..."

He turned, meaning to stride off into the crowd, but Katherine snatched at his sleeve, pulling him back.

"Timothy, wait!"

Chapter Fifteen

Timothy felt like a prize fool. He'd been so careful, not revealing himself, not *speaking*, and now he'd let her name and his voice slip out at once.

She must think I'm the most pompous fool to ever walk the planet, Timothy thought, turning away.

Then he felt cool fingers on his sleeve, brushing his skin.

"Timothy, wait!"

He stopped. Of course he stopped. He could not deny Katherine anything. He never could. Timothy turned, glancing back at her.

She was looking up at him, her expression distant and strangely intent.

"I didn't mean to deceive you," he heard himself say. "I saw you with Mr. Burles, and I..."

"You don't need to apologise," she said, smiling wryly. "It's a masquerade, after all. Half the fun is guessing who is who. Although, you knew who I was at once, didn't you?"

"Of course I did. I'd always know you."

Too much, Timothy, too much.

She removed her hand from his sleeve, now that it was clear he wasn't about to flee into the crowd. Timothy missed its comforting pressure. He longed to dance with her again, to hold her hand in his, see her focused on him above all else. It would be shocking to dance again with a woman so soon, but since they were both masked... well, perhaps tonight was the only night they could get away with it. She lifted her hand, slowly and tentatively, as if she expected him to slip his wrist away at any moment. He felt her fingertips brush the side of his jaw, lifting the mask and gently lifting it away.

"Apollo revealed," she said, so quietly that he almost did not hear it. You said you know me, eh? So, who am I?"

"I beg your pardon?" Timothy managed, not quite able to get enough air into his lungs. "You're Katherine, Lady Katherine Willoughby."

"Ah, but who *am* I?" Katherine said, holding out her arms to indicate the robes, laughing.

"I see. Well, let me think..." he pinched his chin, pretending to consider. "Grecian, of course. A goddess, naturally. I will say... Athena. Am I correct?"

"Yes, perfectly," she laughed. "Athena and Apollo. What a pair!"

"And you really don't mind that I didn't tell you who I was?"

"Not at all. I can't believe you remembered that *Jeremiah's Heart* was my favourite novel. Have you read it yet, by the way?"

He had not. At least, he hadn't read the copy Katherine had lent him. Every word of the novel, however, was burned into his brain.

"Yes," Timothy said, both lying and telling the truth. "I liked it very much. I... I've been thinking about our conversation in the Library, when you said you'd want to meet L. Sterling."

"Yes, I'm sure they're a tremendously interesting person. Imagine the tips they could give, on writing and reading!" Katherine laughed shortly, shaking her head.

Timothy felt as though something were fizzing inside him, getting ready to burst out through his throat, spilling everywhere, impossible to take back.

Don't do it, warned a small voice in his head. *She'll be disappointed to know that you're her revered author. So, so disappointed. Do you want to see her face fall? Do you want to hear her laugh, and not believe you? Do you want to scupper your friendship forever, and go back to scribbling alone at your desk, in the dark?*

He swallowed hard, squeezing his eyes closed. He'd imagined telling her, over and over again. Her reaction was different every time.

Perhaps she would be angry. Perhaps she would be admiring, or skeptical, or shocked, or disappointed. Perhaps a mixture of them all.

"Timothy?"

He opened his eyes to find Katherine looking up at him, brow furrowed. "Are you quite well?" she continued, laying a hand on his arm.

The touch seemed to burn.

"I am," Timothy managed at last. "I had something I wanted to tell you about, something about myself. It may take you by surprise, but I feel that it is something you ought to know."

Serious words, indeed. Katherine blinked, taken aback.

"Oh. Oh, I see. Is it something very worrying, then?"

"No, no. That is... well, I don't know. You see, the thing is..."

"Ah, Lady Katherine! Here you are."

Timothy had never considered himself to be a violent man, but at the moment, he could gladly have knocked Lord Barwood's teeth down his throat.

He saw Katherine's face drop and was obliged to stop talking and turn to face the man swaggering towards them.

Lord Barwood was wearing a rich, burgundy satin outfit, plush and quilted, and a red domino mask hung from his fingers. Apparently he did not want to mar his handsome face with a mask. He smiled indulgently at Lady Katherine, shooting Timothy a poisonous look.

"Cornered by a man in a sheet. Horrifying." He remarked, directing a long, slow look of contempt over Timothy's outfit.

"He's Apollo," Katherine said, a definite edge to her voice.

That did not make it better. Lord Barwood stifled a hoot of laughter.

"Apollo? *Timothy Rutherford*? How ambitious, I must say. And you, my dear Lady Katherine, are none other than the graceful goddess Athena."

He kissed her hand, flashing a confident smile up at her. Katherine did not return it.

"I expect my mother told you who I was," she said shortly, and the confident smile flickered a little.

"I came to ask you to dance," Lord Barwood said, after an awkward pause of half a minute. "They're starting up again. Shall we?"

Timothy said nothing. There wasn't a great deal he could say – Katherine was not permitted to refuse him, after all. She took his arm hesitantly, glancing up at Timothy.

"Goodbye, Timothy. I daresay I'll see you again soon."

"I doubt it, there's a tremendous crush here this evening," Lord Barwood said nastily. "If I were you, Timothy, I'd put the mask back on. Without it, you really do just look like a man in a sheet."

With that parting short, he led Katherine away towards the dance floor, and the crowd quickly swallowed them up.

Timothy did not replace the mask. He didn't bother waiting on the edges of the dance floor either, in an attempt to whisk Katherine away. He'd already made too great of a fool of himself. He'd felt so embarrassingly confident as Apollo, right up until the moment he let Katherine's name slip.

Had she been disappointed, to find his face behind the mask? Had she hoped it was someone else? He searched his memory, but not recall seeing her face drop.

I can but hope.

He weaved his way through the crowd, looking for William. William disliked parties and gathering, and had never had much interest in dressing up, so doubtless he was not having a good time. Timothy had been looking for the best part of half an hour when he saw a familiar black domino lounging on a set of chairs against the wall, glowering at something in the crowd.

"Henry?" Timothy said hesitantly, approaching him. "I didn't know you were here tonight."

"I was obliged to come," Henry Willoughby responded, tearing off his black domino mask. "Just as well, really. Mother is never much use in these situations, William has disappeared, Katherine is cornered by that wretch of an earl, and somebody has to watch *him*."

He nodded into the crowd, and Timothy followed his gaze.

Alexander was propping up the wall by the refreshment table, surrounded by a knot of not-exactly-respectable ladies and gentlemen, all in their cups. It was clear that Alexander was tipsy. His eyes were bright and blurred, and he leaned rather too heavily against the wall. His white domino mask sat askew on his face, and his matching white cloak was stained by what looked like red wine.

That stain won't come out, Timothy thought tiredly. Henry absently patted the seat beside him, and Timothy sat.

They sat in silence for a moment or two. Timothy knew the younger Willoughbys, of course. Alexander was a pleasant young man, if indolent, but Henry was known to be a harder sort of person.

"He's drinking entirely too much," Henry remarked, half to himself. "Ever since the business of the will came out. I know that you know, by the way. William tells you just about everything."

Timothy bit his lip. "You can count on my discretion, you know."

"I know. Have you seen my sister, by the way? With Lord Barwood, I assume."

Timothy swallowed hard. "Yes. They were going to dance together when I left her."

Henry shot him a thoughtful, sideways look, which Timothy did not return.

"She's making a mistake, you know. With the earl."

Timothy stared down at his mask, which now seemed like a second face looking up at him, blank and judgmental.

"Lady Katherine has excellent judgment," he heard himself say. "She will make the best decision for herself, I'm quite sure."

"I'm not sure. She'll make the best decision for the family, which is for her to marry, regardless of who. She's determined, you know. But she doesn't love the earl. He's a wretch. None of us like him, except for Mother. And that's not worth considering, you know. She married Father, after all, and thinks that's what marriages are like. That can't be true, I simply can't believe it."

Timothy began to feel uncomfortable. "Henry, you really shouldn't speak of your parents in that way."

"Why not?" Henry shot back. "My father never did a thing for me. It was as if the three of us didn't exist, only William, and even then, he made Will's life a misery. He made Mother's life miserable too, only she was too foolish to understand what he really was. Or perhaps she did know, and simply became what she had to in order to survive. I shouldn't judge her."

"The late Duke was a hard man, sure enough," Timothy said carefully. "But I have to believe that he cared for his family."

Henry looked him dead in the eyes. "Do you really believe that?"

The answer came at once. *No.*

"Do you intend to travel again, Henry?" Timothy asked, when the pause became unbearable. He considering getting up and leaving, but who else would he talk to? He might risk seeing Katherine and Lord Barwood, and that suddenly seemed a terrible fate.

Besides, Henry was alone, too. He didn't seem any happier than his siblings.

"I don't think I can," Henry said shortly. "I want to stay and see the others settled. I owe them that, at least. If I want my share of the inheritance, I'll need to marry, and then what? Do I leave my wife at home for years on end? What woman would want to travel with me? And if I choose not to marry, I'll be penniless."

"Your siblings would take care of you."

He huffed. "Has it occurred to you, Timothy, that I don't want to live on charity?"

This was quite stinging.

"Of course," Timothy responded sharply. "I know exactly what it's like to make your own way in the world."

Henry had the grace to blush. "I beg your pardon, I forgot about your situation. For what it's worth, I did admire what you did. Leaving home, striking out on your own like that. It's admirable. Few men could manage it. I'm not even sure I could." He sighed, rubbing his eyes. "I never imagined myself marrying. And if I did marry, I thought I would do so in my own time. I would wait until the right person presented themselves. And now, I'm forced into it. Even if I choose to let the deadline elapse, might I not regret it later? Might I not find myself wanting to marry but unable to afford it? I can't expect William to bankroll my travels – even if he is able to marry and get his own slice of the inheritance."

"I... I'm sorry, Henry. None of you deserve this."

Henry shrugged. He seemed tired, all of a sudden. Timothy noticed that his handsome face had lines that his brothers did not – worry lines around the eyes and forehead, signs of tiredness. There were dark circles around his eyes.

As he was considering this, Alexander let out a peal of laughter, and dropped a glass of wine. It shattered at his feet with an enormous tinkling noise, scattering red wine and glass shards everywhere.

The drunken fools all giggled wildly at the mess, laughing at Alexander shaking out the hem of his cloak, which was now stained with red wine like blood.

A poker-faced footman came forward with a brush and shovel and began cleaning up the mess. Timothy saw guests shoot Alexander sharp, disgusted looks, edging away from him.

Beside him, Henry gave a muffled curse, and got to his feet.

"I should try and manage him," he muttered. "I wonder if I can drag him home early."

"Should I get William?"

"If you can find him. Mother was introducing him to scores of ladies, all very keen to meet a handsome young Duke and become the next Duchess, but he didn't seem taken with any of them. The last I saw him, he was trying to get out of the crowd. Good luck to him, that's all I can say."

The conversation was clearly over. Henry got to his feet, roughly tying his mask around his eyes again, more to keep his hair out of his face and his hands free than from anything else. Timothy watched him approach his brother, who was red-faced and laughing uncontrollably now.

"You are drunk, Alexander," Henry hissed, voice low and sibilant. "Come away."

"Oh, let me have a little fun, Henry! Oh, look, there's Timothy. He'll have a drink with us."

"You've had more than enough, you fool. The rest of you, go away. I mean it."

The knot of ladies and gentlemen around Alexander flinched at Henry's tone, glancing at each other, offended. He glared at them until they began to filter away, leaning on each other for comfort. A pool of red wine was beginning to spread out over the floor, spite the poor footman's best efforts. The hem of Alexander's cloak was trailing in it.

This will, this ultimatum, it's driving them all mad, Timothy thought despairingly. *Where on earth will it end? What will they choose – money or love?*

He got up, replacing his mask, and left Henry to wrangle with his younger brother. Diving into the crowd, Timothy began to search for William. Surely he couldn't have gone far.

I have to tell him, Timothy thought, with a flutter of nerves. *I have to tell him how I feel about Katherine. Even if he's shocked, or angry, he needs to know. Perhaps he'll tell me to keep it to myself, in which case I won't have lost anything. Or perhaps he'll say...*

Timothy did not finish the thought.

One thing at a time. Find William first. If you can, of course.

Chapter Sixteen

"... and everybody complimented my Theodosia on her *excellent* watercolours, but then, she does everything with such an excessive degree of accomplishment. It's really a rare thing to see, don't you agree, your Grace?"

William, who was in the middle of smothering a yawn, managed to nod obediently.

His mother had cornered him, in order to introduce Lady Everett and her daughter, Miss Theodosia Figg. Miss Figg was a wan-faced young lady in an unfortunately coloured yellow gown, with no mask or any attempt at a costume. Her mother was a portly lady who talked incessantly and didn't seem to mind in the least that she was the only one talking.

She was the fifth lady – or was it the sixth? He was losing count – who had cornered William and insisted on introducing an eligible daughter or two. Some ladies were clearly not interested in William, and were merely polite, but others seemed keen to secure him. He could almost hear them sounding out their new title in their heads.

It wasn't their fault, he assumed. He knew from Katherine's plight how difficult it was to be a woman in this world. Everything relied on a woman's marriage, and she only had one chance at it. A series of failed relationships or broken engagements could scupper a woman's chance at a future. It was hard to blame them for being so keen to attract a duke, then.

"I see that the dancing is going along nicely," Lady Everett said, eyes boring into William's. "Have you a partner, your Grace? My Theodosia has been bombarded with gentlemen wanting to dance with her; you're quite lucky to find her with an empty set in her dance card. I'm sure you long to dance."

What a subtle hint.

William, however, had had enough.

"I'm afraid not, Lady Everett," he said blandly, acting as if he were too stupid to understand her hint. "I'm quite tired, actually, and entirely too hot. I think I'll take some air. It was so good to see you both. Enjoy the evening, won't you?"

Lady Everett opened her mouth to say something to keep him there, but William did not give her the opportunity. With speed unbecoming of a duke, he turned tail and hurried into the crowd, hastily losing Lady Everett and her accomplished Theodosia.

It's not as if either of them will miss me, he thought wryly.

He hadn't been lying about feeling tired and hot. There was nowhere to sit, not without elbowing one's way through a crowd of people to get to the wall, and even then the seats were mostly occupied with matrons and dowagers, or older gentlemen obliged to escort female relatives. The heat was intense, caused by the press of too many bodies together, of countless candles hanging from the chandeliers, of movement and talk, and William did feel a little faint.

Near the end of one of the supper-rooms, he spotted a half-open French door leading out onto a long balcony. He could almost feel the breeze on his heated skin. Hurrying towards it, William stepped out onto the cool balcony, almost sagging with relief.

The balcony was a long, narrow thing, curving around the side of the house. It was a plain stone walkway, ringed with a chest-high wall, overlooking the lawns and gardens below. Of course, it was too dark to make out much. William moved over to the wall, resting his elbows on the surface and looking down.

He could see the rough silhouettes of shrubs and plants, with a rustling here and there that indicated foxes and rabbits were about. Across the dark lawn, he could see carriage lights in the courtyard, where curricles and gigs were parked, waiting for their occupants to return, the coach drivers guarding them.

I want to go home, he thought dizzily, feeling as miserable as a child. He couldn't go home, of course. He had to stay, to give his siblings a chance to meet people.

Folks were always more open and more *themselves* at a masquerade, in his opinion.

"You know, it's really not proper for us to be here alone."

The unfamiliar voice made him flinch. Stepping away from the wall, he peered down the length of the walkway, near to where it curved around the side of the building. He spotted a woman standing there, barely more than a shadow in the dark.

"I beg your pardon," he said. "I had no idea anyone was out here. I only wanted some air. I'll leave at once, of course."

"No, stay," she said, stepping into the light. "I'd feel terrible if you went back inside and fainted from the heat. It's a terrible crush in there."

The woman was younger than he'd expected, from the dry, cool tone of her voice. William had never been good at estimating ages and judged that she was anywhere between twenty and thirty. She wore a long, quilted blue gown, simply cut, not seeming to be any character in particular. She wore a matching domino mask in the same vibrant blue. Her hair was pinned back neatly, if a little austerely, half covered under a blue cap. Tendrils of red hair escaped. A plain, silver locket hung around her neck, the jewelry not really matching the rest of her clothing. She was pretty, or so he would guess. Full red lips curved up at his scrutiny, as if she guessed what he was thinking.

William flushed and hoped that the darkness hid it.

"I apologise," he heard himself say. "I didn't mean to intrude on your solitude."

"And I didn't mean to intrude on yours," she remarked. She eyed his suit for a long moment, making him wish he'd worn something more elaborate, or at least chosen a mask. "Can I assume you aren't any particular character?"

He winced. "I don't much care for dressing up. Not that I have anything against masquerades, of course, but they aren't really for me."

"Nor me," she said with a sigh, moving over to stand beside him. She rested her elbows on the wall, looking over just as he had done. He caught a whiff of lemon coming from her, an unusual scent. Most ladies smelled of lavender or rosewater, in his opinion.

Not that there was anything wrong with those scents, of course.

She glanced at him out of the corner of her eye, and William blushed red again, a little disconcerted to have been caught staring.

"I don't believe we've been introduced," he said, after a pause.

"No, I don't believe we have."

"I'm Lord William Willoughby, the Duke of Dunleigh."

She turned to face him, smiling that inscrutable smile again. "Yes, I know who you are."

"Oh," he managed, feeling caught off-guard. "You do?"

"Of course I do. Half of the mammas in the crowd today are trying to catch you for their daughters. Half of the daughters want to catch you, too. You're the most eligible man in London."

"I am not."

"Oh, but you are. Handsome, charming, pleasant – you're very personable, *and* you're remarkably wealthy and titled. Any woman would want you."

William thought of the will, and wondered just how many women would want him if they knew his wealth was entirely dependent on walking down the aisle.

"Yourself included, I suppose?" he heard himself say.

Horror immediately set in. That was an entirely inappropriate thing to say to any woman, or any person at all, in any settling. He began to babble.

"Oh, I did not mean... I... forgive me, please, I only meant..."

"No forgiveness needed," she said, chuckling. "I can hardly blame you for being on your guard. But worry not, I have no designs on you. I have no intention of marrying; of that I can assure you. I really did come out here for quiet. Now, I think that I've offended you, so perhaps I will take my leave."

She moved as if to go back inside.

"Stay," William said, before he could stop himself. She glanced back, eyebrows raised questioningly. He bit his lip. "You're rather refreshing," he confessed. "You seem honest, and frankly, I've spent the whole evening being surrounded by people, and yet I feel more alone than ever."

She flashed a quick, hesitant smile. "I know how that feels. Feeling alone in a crowd. It's awful."

She moved back to stand beside him, the two of them resting their arms on the wall and looking out over the dark garden.

"I don't believe I heard your name?" William ventured at last.

"Because I didn't give it," she responded. "Isn't that the point of a masquerade? To guess who's beneath the mask? I knew you at once."

"Yes, but I'm not wearing a mask," he said, feeling just a little piqued. "I don't know. How can I guess your name?"

"A clever man like you could find out. Or perhaps the intention is anonymity. Giving a person a mask is the best and quickest way to find out who they truly are. People will tell you the truth, if they wear a mask. And, of course, if they think they can get away with it."

"You have a cynical view of the world," William observed.

"Perhaps I do. But I'm convinced it's the wrong view. What about you, your Grace? Do you like to see the best in people? Do you believe that with a little courage and love, all the problems of the world can be overcome?"

There was no escaping the derision in her voice, and something else simmered there, too. Bitterness, perhaps? She kept her eyes fixed on the dark horizon, and with the mask and the poor lighting, it was impossible for William to read her face.

"Perhaps that's a simplistic view of the matter," he said at last. "But I do believe in the power of love. Not in the way that novels claim, of course. But let me illustrate. I have three siblings, whom I adore. I would do anything for them, risk anything. At the very moment, I am pursuing marriage, which is all for their good. Left to myself, I would choose differently, but I am willing to sacrifice my own personal happiness to see that my family are safe. If we all took that attitude towards the ones we love, surely the world would be a better place."

She moved to face him, her eyes shadowed.

"I don't doubt that you believe that," she said, after a long pause.

"But… but you don't believe it?"

She bit her lip, glancing back towards the half-open French doors. Heat and light spilled out, along with a flurry of applause and laughter, as the most recent dance came to an end.

"I would like to believe it," she said at last. "I think I really must go."

"Dance with me," William said, before he was even aware of what he was asking. She glanced at him, face blank. He flushed yet again, feeling like an awkward schoolboy.

"I haven't danced at all tonight," he admitted. "I'm not in the mood for it, but it'll look odd if I don't dance at all. And since I'm fairly sure you aren't out to catch me, perhaps you're a safe wager."

She chuckled. "I adore your honesty. But I have no choice, do I? A lady can't turn down an invitation to dance. I'm not sure it even is an invitation, but a request. No, not even that. A demand."

"Well, I am certainly not demanding that you dance with me. I can withdraw my request, if you like, you can simply refuse me, and I'll never breathe a word."

She smiled, shaking her head. "I really believe you would. No, your Grace, I shall dance with you. Let's go inside."

Inside, William watched the reactions of other people to his mystery lady. She had still not revealed her name, and he didn't bother to ask her again. She would tell him if she wanted him to know.

He spotted a thunderstruck Lady Everett in the crowd, with a miserable-looking Miss Figg beside her. There were a few other mammas and their daughters watching him prepare to dance, eyes flitting over to the mystery woman. He saw their gazes narrow and guessed that they did not know who she was, either.

The music began, and so did the dance. William moved mechanically, aware that he had no real grace or even any love for dancing. The blue domino mirrored him, her movements all ostensibly graceful, but without real soul.

"You don't like dancing, do you?" she remarked once, when the dance slowed down enough for them to speak.

"Neither do you," he responded, and earned himself a smile.

"Everybody is looking at us."

"Yes, I haven't danced all night. I said so."

She frowned. "You had better dance with other ladies after me. If I'm the only one you dance with, people will talk."

"I don't mind."

"Perhaps I do."

That silenced him. The dance ended, entirely too soon, which was an unusual thing for William to feel. They bowed and curtseyed to each other, and the dancers exploded in the usual breathless chatter, leaving the dance floor in search of refreshments.

The mystery woman seemed a little on edge now. She had her hands clasped tightly in front of her, and was glancing around, gaze darting here and there but landing on nothing. Gone was the easy confidence she'd shown on the balcony. She seemed smaller, almost.

"Would you like some refreshments?" he asked, inching closer. Somebody in the party would know who she was, and they might come up to introduce themselves.

She flinched, blinking up at him as if she'd almost forgotten he was there.

"I can't, I'm sorry," she said, gaze flicking around again. "I really must go."

"Go? Go where?"

"Leave, what else do you think I mean?" she said, entirely too sharply for a person addressing a duke.

"Let me at least escort you out. Perhaps..."

"No. I am sorry. Thank you for dancing with me, your Grace."

She turned on her heel, diving into the crowd. He heard little outraged exclamations as she pushed her way through, saw people turn, offended, to glare at her, but then she was gone, lost in the sea of people.

He moved to go after her, but a hand on his shoulder stopped him. Flinching, he turned around to see a man wearing long Grecian robes and a large mask.

"It's me, Will," Timothy said, taking off the mask. "I've been looking for you."

Biting his lip, William turned to follow the woman. It was too late, of course. There was no sign of her, as if she'd never been there at all. He sighed, turning back to his friend.

"Timothy, do you know a young woman in a blue domino? Red hair, blue dress, small."

He frowned, shaking his head. "I don't, I'm afraid. What's her name?"

"If I knew her name, I wouldn't be... oh, never mind. I just danced with her, that's all, but I didn't get her name."

"Aren't you meant to be introduced before you... oh, look, William, was that her locket?"

Timothy pointed, and William spotted the glint of silver at once. He dived to collect it, recognizing at once the silver locket the mystery woman had worn around her neck. The clasp on the delicate chain had broken, and she likely hadn't even noticed that her locket was gone.

"I'll have to find out who she is to return it," he murmured. Almost without thinking, William opened the locket.

Inside, there was a single miniature, carefully tucked in. The miniature was of a little boy, curls falling over his forehead, large eyes staring seriously out at the viewer. William frowned down at it.

Timothy was still standing there, looking uncomfortable. "Will? Are you alright? You look ill."

"I feel ill," William mumbled. "I think I want to go home."

"I... I wanted to talk to you about something."

He passed a hand over his face. "Can't it wait, Tim? I really don't feel well."

Timothy swallowed hard, pressing his lips together. "Of course, of course. It can wait."

Nodding absently, William tucked the locket carefully into his pocket, and turned to leave.

Chapter Seventeen

It felt as though Katherine had barely put her head on the pillow before a huge crash downstairs had her jerking awake again.

She sat bolt upright, blinking in the pre-dawn gloom of her bedroom, trying to work out what, exactly, had happened.

The masquerade had gone on long past midnight. William had felt ill, and gone home early in the night, and she had never been able to find Timothy again. That should not have bothered her as much as it did. She had arrived home shortly before one in the morning, exhausted, miserable, and hollow.

The hollow feeling did not stand up to scrutiny. Whenever she asked herself why, exactly, she felt so hollow, it was as if her brain shied away from it. And now here she was, bleary-eyed, exhausted, and not entirely sure if the noise was part of a dream or not.

It was not. The crash came again, followed by an angry voice. Swinging her legs out of bed, Katherine pulled on a dressing-gown and hurried downstairs.

It was easy enough to find the source of the noise.

Alexander lay in the foyer, his white domino suit stained and torn in places. His arms and legs were spread out, like a puppet with the strings cut. An upturned table lay beside him, with a broken vase spread across the floor. The butler, a robe tied tightly around him, was holding up a candle over the miserable scene, looking unsure as to what to do next.

Henry stood over his brother, face red, looking purely furious. He glanced up, briefly meeting Katherine's eye.

"He's drunk," Henry said, somewhat unnecessarily. "He got drunk at the masquerade, and then he went to a club and drank more. I had to drag him out."

"You're no fun, Henry," Alexander slurred. "Why can't I be happy?"

"I don't want to stop you from being happy, fool," Henry snapped. "I just don't want you to have your reputation ruined. Get up, can't you? I want to go to bed, and I can't until you're settled."

Alexander did not seem to hear him. His head rolled back onto the cold floor tiles with a nasty *bang*. Swallowing hard, Katherine hurried down the rest of the stairs.

"Get something to go underneath his head. No, wait, a glass of water," she said, and the butler moved at once. "Henry, let's try and bring him round. If he vomits now, he might choke on it."

Henry's lip curled. "I can't believe he's gotten himself into this state. What would he have done if I wasn't there?"

"Don't think about that now."

"How can I think of anything else? He's always been a bit of a fool, but never like this. I can't keep doing this, Kat."

"You're his brother," she said shortly. "What else should you do?"

That was the wrong thing to say. Henry's pride had always been prickly, and now he was tired, angry, and upset. He recoiled, glaring at her.

"If you're going to be like that, I suppose I should just let you get on with it," he snapped. "I'll go to bed."

He stamped towards the stairs and was halfway up by the time he finally paused, glancing down.

Katherine watched him, too tired to argue.

"I don't want to fight," she said quietly. "But really, what else are we to do? We can have a serious word with Alexander later, but not now. It's pointless, now. And I can't get him upstairs by myself. I need your help."

Henry's shoulders sagged.

"Alright," he muttered. "I'll help. But you must talk to him."

"I'll do my best. Perhaps we should tell William about this."

"Will? Ha. He's not much help these days."

"Leave him be, Henry. William has a lot to think about."

"And the rest of us don't?"

That was an excellent point, and Katherine fell silent.

Between the two of them, they got Alexander more or less up onto his feet, and slowly, step by step, they climbed the stairs. The butler followed behind with a jug of a water and a glass, looking anxious.

"Father would laugh to see us now," Alexander mumbled, barely coherent. "I think he'd be pleased."

"Don't think about Father now," Henry said, teeth gritted. "Concentrate on getting into bed before your sister and brother let you fall down the stairs."

"When you think about it," Alexander said drowsily, "our darling Papa is essentially selling us, isn't he? One might even call it whor…"

"Stop," Katherine said, far too loudly for that time of the day. "Stop it now, Alexander. I mean it. You can't talk like that."

"He's right, though," Henry remarked, and when Katherine looked over, her brother's face was ashen. "That's exactly what Father did. Sold us. Or rather, forced us to sell ourselves, for the price of our inheritance. He must have known how we'd all scramble in a panic, desperate for our money, throwing ourselves at whoever would have us. I wonder if he laughed about it, when the idea first occurred to him."

"He's dead, Henry. There's nothing he can do to us now."

"No, not beyond what he's already done. Do you know, when I went abroad, I thought I'd finally got rid of him. Finally taken a few steps towards freedom. It was thrilling, I can tell you that. Thrilling. I was so happy. And then, this happened. It's almost funny, isn't it?"

"Henry…"

"Look at what he's done to us all. William is falling apart, you're forcing yourself into pursuing a gentleman who isn't worth your spit, Alexander is drinking himself into a stupor to avoid facing the truth, and I'm going to be unhappy forever. Well, all of us are, I suppose."

"I mean it, Henry. Stop."

They reached the top of the stairs. Alexander's room was nearby, and Katherine felt a flood of relief. Henry was mercifully silent as they manhandled Alexander into his room and onto his bed. He was already snoring. They pulled off his cloak and boots and left it at that.

As they turned to go, William appeared in the doorway, in his nightclothes, holding a candle.

"What is it?" he asked, blinking. "What happened?"

"Don't worry about it," Henry said shortly, pushing past him. "You're too late to help, as always."

William flinched, watching Henry stride away down the corridor. He looked back at Katherine hopelessly.

"It's fixed, Will," she said quietly. "Now I want to go to bed. I'm so tired."

He didn't say a word or stop her as she stepped past him and headed along to her room. When Katherine fell into bed, she felt into a deep and dreamless sleep at once.

***

"Lord Barwood is here to see you, Lady Katherine," the butler announced.

Katherine and her mother were sitting in the parlour, quietly employed in their own pursuits. William was in his study, Alexander still in bed, and where Henry could be was anyone's guess.

Katherine winced. "Can you tell him we're not at home, or busy? I really haven't the energy today."

"Don't do that!" the Duchess said, sharply. "What are you thinking of, Katherine? Why would you not receive the Earl?"

She sighed. "Because he's hard work, Mama. I had a late night and a disturbed sleep, and besides, we have Lady Amelia Spencer's soiree tonight. Can't I have a quiet afternoon?"

The Duchess pressed her lips together. She glanced over at the butler.

"Tell Lord Barwood to come into the parlour," she said shortly, ignoring Katherine's sigh. The butler did not look particularly pleased but was obliged to obey.

"I don't care for him, Mama," she said quietly, once the butler was gone.

"It doesn't matter," the Duchess responded, neatly threading her embroidery needle. "He wants to marry you, he's eminently suitable, and you haven't time to be picky. Even if you were picky, what would be wrong with him? He's handsome, rich, and plenty of other ladies are interested in him."

"I don't much care. They can have him."

The Duchess threw down her embroidery. "Well, then, why don't you simply tell him you have no interest in him, and waste away the time you have. Then the entire fortune, which is ours by right, will be lost, your brothers ruined, and you a ridiculous, poor old spinster. Is that what you want, Katherine? Is it?"

Before Katherine could respond, the door opened, and Lord Barwood was introduced. He stepped inside, grinning confidently.

"Lord Barwood!" the Duchess gushed, bouncing to her feet. "What a pleasure. Come in, come in. We'll have some tea ready directly. Did you enjoy the masquerade last night?"

"I did," he said, laughing and settling down on the sofa beside Katherine. "Although some of the costumes were frankly ridiculous. One gentleman – I forget his name – came dressed in a sheet, and said that he was *Apollo*, can you believe it? Ha, ha!"

He shot a quick, sideways glance at Katherine as he said this, indicating that he did remember who it was, after all.

"Well, I was Athena," Katherine found herself saying, "So I think Timothy and I were well-matched."

"Oh, was it young Timothy Rutherford?" the Duchess said, her nose wrinkling delicately. "A pleasant boy, but rather strange. Do you know, he moved out of his family home and took up *apartments*? I've heard they're rather squalid. What is the boy thinking, can you imagine?"

"Well, it serves us to know whose acquaintance we should encourage, and which friendships should be left in the past," Lord Barwood said. His voice was pleasant, but there was an edge to his voice that Katherine did not like. "Do you not agree, Lady Katherine?"

"I think that if a friendship is worth preserving, everything that can be done to preserve it should be done," she said calmly.

This, apparently, was not what Lord Barwood wanted to hear. He pursed his lips, shooting a knowing look at the Duchess. The Duchess gave a little shrug, then picked up her embroidery, pointedly looking away. The implication was clear – she was chaperone only, and Katherine and Lord Barwood would be on their own, conversation-wise.

Wonderful, Katherine thought tiredly.

"Do you recall that gig of mine, Lady Katherine?" Lord Barwood remarked, leaning back against the sofa and spreading out his arms and legs. "The one we went promenading in?"

Katherine did remember being dizzyingly high up, with high-spirited horses plunging here and there, while Lord Barwood laughed and cracked his whip at a few beggars as they trundled by. She remembered hanging on so tight her knuckles stood out white in her hands.

"I recall," she said lightly.

"Well, I broke a spring, can you believe it? Shocking thing. But I have another, similar style, but a little faster, you know. Now that I'm used to the new gig, the old one seems unbearably slow. I must take you out in it. I went so fast around one corner that some old fool of a man, ready to step out into the road, threw himself back with a shout, and landed in a wheelbarrow of manure. It was the funniest thing. I laughed until I was almost sick."

"Was he alright?"

"Eh?" Lord Barwood said, missing a beat.

"The old man. Was he alright?"

"I have no idea. How should I know? I went on, of course – places to be. Served him right for being such a fool."

Katherine jabbed her needle into her embroidery, trying to pretend it was Lord Barwood's hand.

I can't do this, she thought, as he waxed eloquent about his new gig and what he intended to do with it. *I can't marry this man. Who am I fooling?*

But I must. If I don't marry, we lose everything. There's no arguing with that. Father knew this, he did it deliberately. I can't just wait. If the Season ends, I've lost everything. Lord Barwood will marry me, and it's not as if anyone else is courting me.

Can I possibly spend the rest of my life with him? A man who talks of nothing but money and curricles, who makes awful comments about people at parties, and thinks it's funny to run old men off the road?

What is my alternative?

She squeezed her eyes closed when the embroidery started to blur before her eyes. She could not cry. Not here, not in front of this man. She risked opening her eyes, drawing in a few deep, calming breaths, and glanced up.

Nobody had noticed. Lord Barwood was still talking about himself – he was talking about a hunting expedition now, one where he had apparently shot more birds than anyone else and was complimented by all – and the Duchess was absorbed in her sewing.

"Are you going to Lady Amelia's soiree tonight, Lord Barwood?" Katherine said desperately, interrupting him.

His eyes tightened at the interruption, but he composed himself and smiled indulgently.

"Yes, I believe so. You ladies and your soirees! I'm afraid you'll be obliged to talk with Timothy Rutherford again, since he is the lady's nephew."

"I don't mind, I like Timothy," Katherine said firmly. The Duchess' head went up, eyes flashing a warning. Katherine ignored it and continued. "We have the same taste in novels, you see, and a great deal in common. We've known each other since we were children."

Lord Barwood eyed her, clearly annoyed. "I imagine you're just like brother and sister, then," he said bluntly. "As if he were William, or Alexander."

Katherine smiled smoothly. "That's not at all how it is."

Lord Barwood sniffed, displeased. "Hm. Well, I came to see if you wanted to dance tonight, but I have just recalled that Lady Amelia will almost certainly not have dancing, or indeed anything fun, at this dreadful party of hers. I had better go."

He rose to his feet, and the two women politely rose along with him.

"I'm sure we'll keep each other entertained," the Duchess said, but Lord Barwood would not be soothed. He grunted a goodbye and left at once. When he'd gone, the Duchess rounded on her daughter.

"Why did you say all that nonsense about Timothy? You know how jealous men get!"

"It's not my concern."

"Do you really want to spend the whole evening talking to Timothy? No, you do not! So, Katherine, I would advise you to hold your tongue, and don't you dare drive Lord Barwood away! Sometimes I think you are entirely too stubborn for your own good."

The Duchess sat down with a thump, sniffing in annoyance, and began to angrily stab at her embroidery. Katherine sat too, but now she felt dizzy and strange.

The simple answer was that she *would* like to spend the evening talking to Timothy. They never seemed to run out of things to talk about, or ever really feel uncomfortable with each other. In fact, he was the only person she was looking forward to seeing at the soiree tonight.

She was not entirely sure what to do with this revelation. Swallowing hard, Katherine turned her attention back to her embroidery, but barely got beyond lifting the needle.

Am I falling in love with Timothy? She wondered, with a flutter. *And if I am, what on earth am I going to do?*

Chapter Eighteen

The relief on Amelia's face when she saw Timothy made him glad that he had come after all.

"Oh, Timmy, you're here! You came! I'm so pleased!" Amelia whispered, fluttering towards him.

The guests weren't meant to be arriving for another half hour or so, but the house was already prepared for them. In the background, Timothy saw Rebecca lounging in the drawing room, with Christopher and his wife looking bored beside her. Lady Rustford was there, of course, but no sign of Lord Rustford.

That made sense. He would never lower himself to attend a party thrown by his spinster sister-in-law. No doubt he'd taken himself out to his club as early as possible and was congratulating himself on a lucky escape at this very moment.

"Of course I came," Timothy said, hooking his arm through his aunt's. "Did you think I wouldn't?"

"Oh, I don't know. I can never tell with you sometimes, Tim. Come on, come through to the library, that's where we're sitting. Some of the ladies seemed quite excited about the literary discussions this evening, what do you think?"

"I think that sounds interesting. Can I assume that the ladies of your book club are coming?"

"Indeed you can," Amelia said, laughing. "Now, come on and take a look at the library, and tell me what you think. I spent hours on it."

Timothy followed his aunt into the library, which was alight with candles, decorated with flowers and garlands, books laid out invitingly on tables. She had arranged groups of chairs so that people could sit together in small groups, and the pianoforte stood on a platform in the corner, the piano stool pulled out just a little in case anybody fancied playing music. A fire crackled invitingly in the hearth.

"What do you think?" Amelia asked anxiously. "Does it look pleasant enough? Constance stuck her head in and laughed. She said that it looked like a spinster's paradise."

Timothy briefly entertained a fantasy of upending a jug of wine over his sister-in-law's head.

"Constance wouldn't know a pleasant-looking gathering if it landed directly on her head. This is lovely, Amelia. And I know that you don't host very often, so everybody will be excited on that account, in any case. This is all lovely, thank you. Is the dinner all prepared?"

"Oh, yes, I had a long talk with the cook yesterday. Nothing too heavy, and I thought we could start with that delicious soup she made the other week, the one that..."

Amelia trailed off into a long discussion of the food they would be eating, and the various courses she'd decided upon. Timothy listened good-naturedly, grinning down at her. It was good to see Amelia so animated. All too often, the poor woman seemed almost overshadowed by her overbearing family. Timothy knew exactly how that felt. The difference was that Amelia did not have the opportunity to move away and start up her own life.

Unlike Timothy, she truly was trapped.

Amelia paused for breath, and he glanced down at her, a lump rising to his throat. She smiled uncertainly up at him, and he wondered whether she knew what he was thinking after all.

"It's lovely, Amelia," Timothy said at last. "I'm looking forward to it very much."

Amelia beamed, something like relief tinging her features. "I'm so glad, Timmy. I'm so glad. Oh, is that a knock at the door? People must be arriving! I'd better go and greet them. You wait here!"

She scurried along the corridor, leaving Timothy alone. He drew in a deep, fortifying breath, and pasted on a polite Society smile to greet the guests.

***

So far so good.

One hour later, the guests were almost all there, excluding a few stragglers. The room was full of laughter and muted conversation, along with the clinking of glasses. A young lady and gentleman had seated themselves at the piano and were playing a genteel little duet, pitched low to add to the ambience. A few guests had taken themselves off into quiet corners to read and seemed entirely content with their choices in the matter.

Standing by the hearth, sipping his champagne, Timothy was perfectly placed to observe the room. Lady Rustford sat nearby with her son and daughter-in-law, looking thoroughly bored, but everybody else seemed to be having a good time. Amelia was surrounded by clumps of her friends, chatting eagerly, laughing, and generally seeming comfortable.

Timothy allowed himself a small smile. He would make his excuses and leave shortly after dinner, once it was sure that Amelia's party would be considered a success.

"Ah, Timothy, there you are."

Ice tingled down his spine. Timothy swallowed hard, turning to see Katherine standing near him. There was a faint smile on her face, and an odd, unreadable expression in her eyes. The old, familiar nerves arced through his stomach.

"Lady Katherine, what a pleasure."

She inclined her head. "I saw you as soon as I arrived, but I haven't had leisure to speak to you. Now, I came to find you because we're all talking about L. Sterling novels, and my friend Kitty claims that men have no sensibilities and can't appreciate a good novel. At once I informed her that she was incorrect, that *you* appreciate a good novel, and I'm not sure she believes me. So, would you like to come and join us?"

Timothy smiled. "I would, thank you."

A matching smile spread over Katherine's face. She was still watching him, a strange and inscrutable expression in her eyes. Their gazes held for a heartbeat too long, certainly longer than was proper. There were *rules* in Society as to how long a lady and gentleman should be looking at each other.

Timothy dropped his gaze first, breaking the spell. He immediately regretted it.

Coward, he thought wearily. *Can't even look her in the eyes for more than a moment. Ridiculous to think that you once considered telling her how you felt about her. She'd laugh in your face.*

His maudlin reflections were interrupted by Katherine's gloved hand sliding through the crook of his elbow.

"Come on, then," she said lightly, just a hint of a tremor underneath her voice. "Let's go and meet the others."

***

"My favourite L. Sterling books *have* to be the *Rosalie* books," one lady, the aforementioned Kitty, said with firmness. "They're simply perfect. They have everything – adventure, romance, suspense – perfect."

"I agree," Katherine put in, "but I do believe that some of the older works have more of the spirit which captured us all in the beginning. Don't you agree, Timothy?"

Timothy was feeling, to put it lightly, out of his depth. He'd heard so much praise heaped on his books in the past hour that he felt as though he were listening in on a conversation to which he were not invited. He was sure that his face was bright red.

"I... I'm not sure what you mean."

"Oh, yes you do," Katherine laughed. "The excellent way in which the author writes female heroines, for one. That's why so many of us are *sure* that L. Sterling is a woman. How else could a writer get into a woman's head? What do you all think?"

"I agree," Kitty said stoutly. "Impossible for the writer to be a man."

"Although," Timothy managed weakly, "perhaps the author – if it *were* to be a man – were simply a man who observed the world around him, and viewed women as individuals in their own right, and equal to a man. Perhaps he has female friends and relatives who provide him with the inspiration for his characters."

"It's not *impossible*," Kitty admitted begrudgingly, "But *highly* unlikely, I'm sure."

Timothy bit his lip. "If the author were revealed to be a man, would that disappoint you all?"

There was a heartbeat of silence.

"No," Katherine responded slowly. "No, because it would not undo the magic of the books. I suppose for us – myself, especially – we want to see notable female authors in the world. I know critics don't take novels seriously, but I believe that novels and works of fiction are the future. No matter how hard all these serious critics and deep thinkers try to belittle novels, convincing us that ladies of serious minds should not bother themselves with such nonsense, we all still love them. People love novels, and for me, at least, L. Sterling embodies the growing movement of novel-reading. So many other authors, wonderful though they are, only release a few books, which are read voraciously, then there's no more. L. Sterling, on the other hand, releases novel after novel, each one perfect, each one different. It's remarkable."

There was a brief moment of silence after this speech. Timothy swallowed hard, horrified to notice that he felt rather shaky.

"I see," he managed at last. "That's very well put, Lady Katherine."

"Now," Kitty said, when the silence had dragged on a little more, "are we going to discuss our theories for the latest *Rosalie* book? When *will* it be released? I'm going mad, waiting."

Before anything else could be said, a door slammed, loud enough to cut through all the chatter, and echoing footsteps sounded along the hallway.

Timothy felt as if he knew who it was before the door even opened.

"Apologies for my lateness, everybody!" Lord Barwood announced breezily, stepping into the room. "I do hope you'll all forgive me."

He made a half-hearted bow to Amelia, barely glancing her way, and immediately made his way across the room to sit beside Katherine. Kitty was obliged to shuffle along the bench, to avoid being sat on.

Lord Barwood shot a quick, intense look of dislike towards Timothy, then beamed falsely around the circle.

"So, what are we all talking about?"

"We are talking about L. Sterling and their novels," Katherine said, her voice cool.

She doesn't like him, Timothy realised, with a flutter.

Lord Barwood scoffed, letting out a harsh laugh. "Oh, that sensationalist fool? Good lord, ladies, surely you are not going to let your clear minds be sullied by such nonsense?"

"Do you read L. Sterling's novels, then?" Kitty asked acidly.

"Lord, no. I don't bother myself with novels at all. It's trite stuff, though, ain't it? That's what everyone says. Oh, and they are all claiming that the author is a woman. I laughed and laughed when I heard that. Of course it's a woman – no man would ever debase himself to scribble such nonsense, ha-ha!"

There was a painfully long pause after this comment. After all, aside from Timothy and Lord Barwood, the circle was made up entirely of women. Katherine sat bolt upright, not looking at anyone in particular, seeming entirely mortified.

"Each to their own," Timothy said placidly. "Although you're in poor company here, then. We all enjoy novels, and I think you might find yourself outnumbered in that respect."

Lord Barwood gave a half-laugh, as if he suspected a joke, but a quick glance around the faces of the others revealed otherwise. His expression soured.

Before the atmosphere could grow more uncomfortable, Amelia rose to her feet, clapping for attention.

"Ladies and gentlemen, I do hope you've all enjoyed your musical and literary discussions half as much as I have enjoyed listening to them. Supper is now ready, so if you would all like to make your way through to the dining room, we'll start eating soon."

There was a general buzz of conversation and activity, with people rising to their feet and preparing to leave. Ladies had to be escorted through, of course, and gentlemen had to find ladies to escort, so there was a general pairing-up before anyone could turn towards the door.

Timothy was a heartbeat too slow. He turned back from Amelia, who was being escorted by a yellow-haired gentleman, and saw Lord Barwood offering his arm to Katherine, grinning shrewdly.

With something like resignation, Katherine took his arm. Lord Barwood shot a quick glance at Timothy, as if reassuring himself that Timothy *was* watching and knew fine well that he was being snubbed. The two of them glided past, the rest of the party more or less paired up by now. Timothy followed the crowd out into the hallway, alone.

Chapter Nineteen

Katherine quietly seethed with rage. Who did he think he was, being so dismissive about their favourite author?

There were plenty of lively debates going on in the library, of course there were, but only between people who'd actually *read* the works of the author they were talking about. To sit down in a group of literary experts and so casually call all novels 'trite stuff' and 'such nonsense' – well, it was unbearable. Katherine had seen the expression on her friends' faces and had almost been ready to sink with embarrassment on Lord Barwood's behalf.

Not that *he* seemed embarrassed, of course. Oh, no, not he. Why would he care, even for an instant, about the opinions of a group of women? Unmarried women, most of them.

And Timothy, of course.

Despite herself, despite the necessity to stay cool and composed with so many eyes on her, Katherine allowed herself a small smile. Timothy had been... well, he had been wonderful. He'd been kind, listened carefully, hadn't interrupted any of the ladies, and after all that, he really did have something useful to add to the conversation.

In fact, he'd had them all listening agog when he talked about writing techniques. In fact, Katherine was beginning to wonder whether he might have turned *his* hand to writing before, he seemed to know the industry so well.

Timothy would write an excellent book, she thought to herself. *And I'm sure it would be a novel.*

"You seem preoccupied," Lord Barwood remarked, filing through into the dining room with the rest of the guests. "Penny for your thoughts, my dear."

Katherine clenched her jaw. "My thoughts are worth more than that, I think."

"Oh, I doubt it."

She shot a quick, outraged glance up at him, but Lord Barwood's expression was smooth, and he was looking away.

Had... had she imagined it? Surely he wouldn't have said something so shockingly rude, not to her face. Surely not.

There were no set places around the table, so the guests were sitting down wherever they liked. That meant that there was no excuse to prevent Katherine from sitting beside Lord Barwood. She sank miserably into the seat he pulled out for her, the last of her hope fizzling away. She'd spend the rest of the meal fielding Lord Barwood's conversation, and probably the rest of the night, too. The man would stick to her side like glue.

And then a man sank into the seat beside her, and her heart leapt.

"Ah, Timothy," Katherine said, smiling wider than she should have done. "We finally have the opportunity of sitting beside each other. I'm glad."

"So am I," Timothy admitted. "I had to bargain with Mrs. Flynn to get this seat."

"I shall promise you scintillating conversation in return."

Timothy chuckled at that, earning himself a glare from Lord Barwood. Timothy only stared right back, unmoved.

Lord Barwood sniffed, dropping his gaze first.

The first courses were served, the usual fare a person would expect at a party like this – good soup and bread, followed by delicate roasted meats and vegetables, nothing too complicated, but all very tasty. The butler and the footmen silently circled the table, filling up wine glasses wherever possible.

Already, Lord Barwood had drunk two glasses.

Not a very auspicious start, Katherine thought, watching him swig back the last dregs of his third glass and gesture at the butler to fill it again.

"Well, Mr. Rutherford," Lord Barwood said, setting down the wine glass with a too-loud *clack*. "Tell me more about this love of novels you have. I don't believe I've ever met a man who reads novels."

"Actually, I would say that you haven't met a man who *admits* to reading novels," Timothy replied coolly. Katherine was obliged to lean back in her seat to let the two men speak over her. It wasn't exactly good manners to speak over a fellow dinner guest, but that was neither here nor there now, frankly.

"No?"

"No," Timothy affirmed. "Thinking of the style of company you keep, Lord Barwood, I would say that you simply don't know any men who *can* read."

There was a taut silence. Katherine pressed her napkin over her mouth to hide her smile.

"I beg your pardon?" Lord Barwood snapped.

Timothy smiled beatifically. "Just a little joke, Lord Barwood."

The man grunted. "Not very funny. It's not particularly manly, is it? Novel-reading."

"Why not?"

Lord Barwood blinked, glancing at Katherine as if she had the slightest inclination to help him get out of the conversational hole he'd dug himself into.

"Eh?"

"Why not, Lord Barwood?" Timothy repeated, leaning forward. "Why should it be unmanly to read novels? Plenty of men have *written* them. What's wrong with reading them?"

"Yes, yes, but the men who write novels write them for ladies to read."

"And that somehow makes a difference, does it?"

Lord Barwood blinked. It was clear that the man wasn't used to being called upon to justify himself, and he was not enjoying it now.

He glanced at Katherine, who flashed a tight-lipped smile.

"Timothy makes a very good point, Lord Barwood."

Lord Barwood snarled. "He makes no point. No point at all. Novels are nonsense, everybody knows that. If ladies want to entertain themselves with nonsense, that is their concern. I, for one, would not allow the future Lady Barwood to fill her head with such nonsense. No man of sense would want his wife feeding on such nonsense."

"What kind of nonsense are you referring to, Lord Barwood?" Timothy asked sweetly. "After all, you don't read novels yourself."

"Oh, you know the sort."

"No, actually, I don't. Do you, Lady Katherine?"

"I'm quite at a loss," Katherine remarked. She was beginning to enjoy herself. Lord Barwood was going red. Hopefully he was regretting plonking himself next to her, and perhaps he would rethink monopolizing her attention for the rest of the evening.

"The sort of things novelists write about. Women being forced into marriages and running away, and goodness knows what else, when everybody knows that parents who arrange their daughters' marriages generally choose better than the woman herself."

"Is that so?" Katherine muttered, taking a long sip of her wine. "Why do you think somebody else would choose a woman's husband better than she could?"

He blinked at her. "Are you in earnest?"

"Deadly earnest."

"Well, it stands to reason. Ladies think with their hearts. They're all emotion, and don't think of logic at all."

"I'm not sure you know enough ladies to make such a sweeping statement."

Lord Barwood shifted, irritated. He was clearly sick of the conversation, and it was visibly grating on him that Katherine and Timothy would not let him drop the matter. She shot a quick glance over her shoulder at Timothy, the two of them exchanging knowing glances.

"It's simply scientific fact, Lady Katherine," Lord Barwood blustered. "And besides, I know quite well that most ladies pick their own husbands. The Season is designed for such a thing, after all. The problem with modern women, you see, is that they do not appreciate the freedom they have. You hear such nonsensical requests – women wanting to vote, wanting to engage in *professions*, for heaven's sake – and frankly, it infuriates me. Women have great freedom in this part of the world. Imagine if these dissatisfied women lived in a part of the world, they were obliged to cover their heads all the time. How would they feel *then*?"

"It is custom for a lady to wear a bonnet whenever she ventures outside," Katherine pointed out equably. "There are a great many rules regulating what a lady can and cannot do, and what she must wear."

"That is not the same. And *voting* is a frankly nonsensical thing. Imagine, trusting a silly young woman with a *vote*? Can you imagine it?"

Katherine sighed. "I can imagine it, Lord Barwood."

The conversation finally trailed away. Lord Barwood was clearly piqued at the subject and shot numerous wounded little glares at Katherine. He tried to ignore Timothy altogether.

The dinner dragged on through several more courses, and Katherine contented herself with talking to Timothy instead. Lord Barwood probably fancied himself to be punishing her by ignoring her, but in truth, it was a huge relief.

Towards the end of the dessert course, Amelia came flitting around the table, and tapped Katherine on the shoulder.

"I'm asking some of the younger people if they'd like to play a few songs on the pianoforte after dinner," she whispered. "Would you mind joining in?"

"Of course I will. Is there music?"

"Yes, there is. Would you mind going first? Just a few songs will do, or even just one – whatever you feel comfortable with."

Katherine smiled at Amelia and nodded. It meant that she wouldn't have much chance to speak to Timothy, but it also meant that Lord Barwood would be obliged to leave her alone. Although perhaps his ill-temper would continue into the evening. If she talked exclusively about novels with her friends, he might go away.

Amelia fluttered away to another one of the young people, leaving Katherine alone between the two gentlemen. She glanced first at Lord Barwood, then at Timothy.

How strange that two men of a similar age could be so different. How seeing one could make my heart sink, and seeing the other could make me feel... well, make me feel entirely different.

***

It was entirely an accident when Katherine learned that Timothy was leaving. She was just stepping down from the pianoforte to polite applause, with another lady stepping up after her, when she saw his familiar head bobbing through the crowd, towards the exit. She hurried after him, hand outstretched to touch his arm.

He stopped abruptly, and Katherine nearly walked into his back. It left them standing entirely too close together.

"You… you're going?" Katherine stammered. "So soon?"

Timothy flushed. "I'm sorry, I didn't mean to leave so early. I just received word that my father is on his way home. He'll summon me to his study to receive a lecture as soon as he gets back – that's his way. It's better if I leave before he arrives. I've explained it all to Amelia, and she understands. Between you and me, my father is almost certainly in his cups, and few things inspire rage in him like my presence. I am sorry – but at least I was able to stay for your pianoforte performance. It was excellent, by the way, but I fear I am pushing the limits of timeliness."

Katherine bit her lip. He'd risked running into his wretched father, just so that he could hear her play the pianoforte? Even after he'd heard her play the pianoforte countless times over the years.

"I see. Well, I'm sorry for it – I look forward to our discussions."

Timothy's breath seemed to stop in his throat. He eyed her for a long moment, long enough for his gaze to make Katherine's skin prickle.

"Really? You do?"

She nodded, not entirely sure why her throat had suddenly turned as dry as it had.

"That… that means a great deal to me, Katherine."

Timothy reached out, tentatively, and she felt his fingers brush hers.

"You mean a great deal to me."

Had she really said that? Aloud? How delightfully shocking."

"I..." Timothy began, then stopped, brow furrowing. "Oh, now isn't the time."

He turned to leave, but Katherine grabbed at his arm again.

"Wait. Before, you'd said that there was something you wanted to talk to me. Do you remember? You never did tell me what it was."

Timothy swallowed reflexively. He seemed nervous, and Katherine couldn't for the life of her work out why. Had she said something wrong?

"I... now isn't the time, Katherine, I'm sorry. I'll explain it all another time."

"Oh," Katherine was aware of a sense of disappointment coursing through her. "That's quite alright, of course."

Timothy gave a sharp nod, backing away as if he were afraid that he would change his mind if he lingered. Katherine stayed where she was, staring down the hall after him.

Why did she feel as if everyone worth talking to at this party had just gone? Why did she feel hollow and miserable?

Oh dear, Katherine thought tiredly. *I think I may be in love with Timothy.*

Then she heard Lord Barwood call her name and was conscious of a comically intense surge of rage.

Chapter Twenty

William turned the locket over and over in his fingers, as though some new clue might be gleaned from its familiar silver surface.

He kept wondering whether something might click, whether he would look at the little boy's miniature inside and get some new clue as to who his mother might be, but no. Nothing.

He set the locket down on his desk with a sigh and rubbed his face. This time of day was William's favourite – nobody was around, and he could get work done in the early hours before breakfast. Right now, the rest of them were still in bed. Katherine had attended a party thrown by Timothy's aunt, which was said to have been a great success, so it was fair to assume she would be sleeping for a while longer.

It always made him feel better, getting some work done before they all sat down to eat together. As if he had *earned* his food, somehow.

Of course, if he did not get his inheritance soon, there would be no work to do, because he would have no money for anything. Everybody knew that estates such as his required a certain amount of money to keep it afloat. They weren't in immediate difficulties, and would likely manage to keep themselves going for a year, perhaps two, but after that...

William deliberately nipped off the thought. There was no point worrying about his own inheritance until Katherine's was all managed. Certainly, pursuing strange women in blue dresses and masks should be *very* far down the list indeed.

Anyway, nobody knew who the woman was. He'd asked around, described her, even showed the locket – so that word might get back to her that somebody had her necklace and was ready to return it – but nobody seemed to have a clue who she might have been.

He had considered asking the hostess of the party that night to provide him with a list of invited guests, but that really was just a step too far. Besides, it wouldn't do him much good. There would be a hundred people there whose names he didn't recognize.

A tap came on the door, and William flinched, as if he'd been caught doing something embarrassing.

"Yes, who is it?" he said at once, sliding the necklace under a pile of papers.

Ruth, the butler, cracked open the door. He looked less than pleased.

"Your lordship, Lord Geoffrey Barwood is here to see you."

"Lord Barwood? So early? It isn't even breakfast."

Ruth pursed his lips. "Shall I tell him to come back later, your lordship?"

William sighed. "Tempting, but no. Show him in, please. And bring some tea, won't you?"

"Very good, your lordship."

Ruth bowed and retreated, leaving William with a minute or two to compose himself. He double-checked that the locket was hidden – something kept him from asking Lord Barwood about the woman – and just had time to paste on a polite smile before the door opened again, and Lord Geoffrey Barwood swaggered in.

"Morning," he said, flinging himself into the chair opposite William's desk without waiting to be asked. "Wasn't sure if you'd be up or not. I see you managed to avoid that heinous party last night."

William lifted his eyebrows. "Lady Amelia Spencer's party? I heard it was very successful. Katherine had an excellent time."

"Humph. I'm sure she would. No, it was nonsense, I'm afraid. Not even any dancing. They just talked about books a great deal. I was bored almost to tears. Still, one must do one's duty, eh?"

"Of course," William said, forcing a quick smile. The more he saw of Lord Barwood, the less he liked him. The man seemed to have that effect on most people. "I'm afraid it's far too early to pay calls on Katherine this morning. I believe she's still in bed. If you wanted to call back later..."

"No, it's you I came to see, old boy," Lord Barwood said disinterestedly, inspecting his nails. "Do you have a moment to talk?"

"Yes, I do," William said reluctantly. "I've ordered tea."

"Tea? At this time of the morning? No, thank you. Have you any brandy?"

"No, I'm afraid not," William lied. "What's the matter?"

"It's good news, all good news, don't worry," Lord Barwood said, laughing. "It is about Katherine, though. I think I've made my intentions quite clear regarding her. Courtship, one would call it. There's an understanding between us. I flatter myself I've been sufficiently clear, and she's a bright enough girl to take my meaning, I think."

"Yes, I understand."

"Not everyone has," Lord Barwood remarked, huffing. "There has been one gentleman in particular who doesn't seem to understand the rules of the game, you know. Once a gentleman has laid claim to a lady, it behoves other gentlemen to back off, you know."

William shifted in his seat, clearing his throat. "Well, the lady is a *person*, you know, not a thing to be won."

Lord Barwood gave a bark of amused laughter. "Just so, just so! Very funny, Will, very funny indeed. Well, I digress. That fellow's opinions mean nothing at all. The less said, the better – I believe he's an acquaintance of yours. But no matter, I've secured her understanding, I think, and I've made it very clear in the eyes of the world what my intentions are to our Lady Katherine. All very proper, within the right amount of time. I've been careful, I can promise you that."

"Th-thank you," William managed, not entirely sure how to take that comment. Lord Barwood dropped him a wink that he could not interpret, so he gave him a hesitant smile, instead.

"I'd like to marry her," Lord Barwood said brusquely. "Lady Katherine, that is. I would like to marry her, so here am I. What do you say?"

There was a heartbeat of silence.

It wasn't an *entirely* unexpected conversation. William could see that Lord Barwood was pursuing Katherine – just like the rest of Society could see it – and it wasn't beyond the realms of possibility that the man would come and request permission to address her.

"You're asking my permission to approach her?" he said at last.

Lord Barwood frowned. "I've already been approaching her, at just about every party we both attended. I even went to a few painfully dull events because I knew she was there, and I wanted to speed along the process as much as it could be sped up. I'm asking your permission to *marry* her."

"Yes, yes, I know that, but I suppose what I mean is, what has Katherine said?"

"Beg your pardon?"

"Well, when you asked her to marry you, I assume she gave her consent?"

Lord Barwood pursed his lips together. It looked very much as if he were trying not to laugh.

"My dear boy, do you think I would approach her *before* getting your consent? You're her guardian, yes? The family head? Yours is the permission I need."

"Well, be that as it may, you do also need Katherine's permission, too. It's her you'll be marrying."

Lord Barwood chuckled. He lifted his marble-topped cane, inspecting the surface closely. "All is in hand, sir, all is in hand. I don't mean to brag, but I do think I'm the finest suitor she'll get."

William bristled. "What is that supposed to mean?"

Lord Barwood spread out his hands apologetically. "Well, she's a pretty girl, and she'll be a rich one, but she is rather outspoken. She attends circulating libraries, she studies, she's... she's a bluestocking, you know. Gentlemen can't stand that. She's a pleasant girl, and will make an admirable wife and mother, but you can't blame men for wondering otherwise, when they see all of that. So much *reading*, you know. My father always said that too much reading addled a girl's brain, and I daresay he's right."

There was a tense silence between them.

"You can't imagine I'm happy to sit here and listen to you criticise my sister," William managed at last. "This is a strange way to try and get my permission, I must say."

Lord Barwood didn't seem particularly bothered by this. He shrugged, twirling his cane in his hands.

"As you like, dear boy, as you like. To be truthful, I don't believe that you *will* deny your consent. You know I'm a fine match, and if you had no intention of my marrying your sister, I think you wouldn't have let us spend so much time together in public. My coming here is really the culmination of what Society has expected for some time."

William bit his lip. It was hard to argue with that.

In the silence that followed, there was a tiny creak outside the closed study door. Lord Barwood didn't seem to have noticed, but William did. He frowned at the door, noticing a shadow shifting underneath.

Was this the right thing for Katherine? William couldn't stop asking himself that question. The fact was – and it was much easier to acknowledge and accept when the man was sitting right in front of him – he did not like Lord Geoffrey Barwood. It seemed that most people didn't. The man was stuck up, overbearing, unkind, dismissive of others, and entirely rude.

William, for one, did not enjoy his company.

But hadn't Katherine been encouraging him? The young lady could have dismissed him with a reprimand if she so desired, William was sure of it. But the fact was that Katherine had to marry, or else the family was doomed. Perhaps she'd settled on Lord Barwood a while ago. It wasn't as if there was anyone else.

Or was there?

William wasn't a fool. He knew that the mysterious, troublesome gentleman that Lord Barwood was talking about was none other than Timothy. William had noticed Timothy and Katherine together more frequently these days. Timothy had always been *his* friend, but now it seemed like his old friend only had eyes for Katherine. He had suspected briefly that Timothy had a fancy for Katherine before now, but then he never *did* anything about it, so what was a man meant to conclude?

Katherine does seem to light up around him, William conceded. *But... but what if Timothy never makes an offer? What if I'm wrong? What if I encourage her to wait for him, and it never happens? I'll doom us all.*

"Well?" Lord Barwood prompted, voice deceptively soft. "You're giving this a great deal of thought."

William sighed. At the end of the day, Katherine was her own woman and could make her own decisions.

"Very well, Lord Barwood. I'll give my consent."

"Excellent! The correct choice, I fancy," Lord Barwood bounced to his feet, to all intents and purposes getting ready to go, and William stretched out a hand to forestall him.

"Wait just a moment."

"Yes?"

"Lord Barwood, I understand that you haven't gone to my sister about this proposal yet."

"Of course not. Your consent is what must be got."

William pressed his lips together. "I've given it, but you must talk to Katherine about this. Get *her* consent."

"I rather assumed you would mention it to her," Lord Barwood drawled, looking faintly annoyed. "I'm going to dine here tonight, after all. You can discuss it before then."

William shook his head. "This is between my sister and you. As the head of the family, I can certainly give my consent to her marriage, but you must speak to *her* about it before anything can be done, do you understand?"

Lord Barwood eyed William for a moment, his expression speculative. Then he flashed a wide, insincere smile.

"Oh, but of course! Don't you fret, William. I'm aware that you have a great deal to concern yourself with. A young duke like yourself must be busy, busy, busy. I shall take Katherine off your hands, and you can be easy in your mind about her. We are brothers now, you see."

William opened his mouth to say that he already had brothers, but Lord Barwood swaggered right out of the study, leaving the door swinging, not even bothering with a goodbye.

Pressing his lips together, William sat back in his chair, trying to fight off the feeling that he'd just made a terrible mistake.

If I have made a mistake, he thought, *all that will happen is that Katherine will turn him down when he makes his proposal. That's all. Nothing to worry about. It won't go too far, surely.*

The butler appeared in the doorway, holding a tea tray set for two. He looked disgruntled.

"Your guest is gone, sir?"

William sighed. "Fortunately, yes. For now, at least."

Chapter Twenty-One

Katherine was pinning up her hair for the morning when a tap came on her bedroom door.

"Who is it?" she called, mouth full of pins. It seemed silly to drag her maid away from her work only to help pin up Katherine's hair for breakfast with her family.

"Only me, Kat."

"Oh. Morning, Alexander. I'm surprised you're up so early. You can come in, I'm decent."

The door creaked open, and Alexander padded inside, closing the door after him. Katherine concentrated on her hair, watching Alexander's reflection settle himself on the edge of the bed.

"So," she said neutrally, after a few moments of silence. "I can tell you have something to say, so let's hear it."

Alexander drew in a steadying breath. "Fine. Lord Barwood visited this morning. He just left. He went to see William."

A shiver went down Katherine's spine. She concentrated on pinning a knot of hair at the nape of her neck. "Oh?"

"He wants to marry you," Alexander said bluntly. "I know that because I listened at the door while they were talking."

"Oh, *Alex*. Eavesdropping never did anyone any good."

"Perhaps not. But I regret nothing. I don't think William enjoyed the conversation. Lord Barwood is an awful man. He's entitled, he's cruel, he believes he's above everyone around him. I can't stand the fellow, and I don't know how *you* can. He wanted William's consent to your marriage, and I think he expected William to broker the match, too."

Katherine pursed her lips. "Yes, I could imagine that. What did William say?"

"He gave his consent, but he told Lord Barwood he would have to talk to you himself and propose. The man didn't seem happy about that, but Will was firm."

"I'm glad," Katherine murmured, laying down the leftover pins. Her hair was secure enough. Maybe a little too tight. It was pulling on her scalp.

She met her brother's eyes through the mirror. Alexander was watching her expectantly.

"Well?"

"Well, what, Alex?"

Alexander sighed. "You can't be about to marry that man. You just can't, Kat."

"Why not?"

"Because he's vile. We all hate him. Even William didn't want to give his consent."

"But he did," Katherine said flatly. "That means that he thinks I should just get it over with. Remember, once I'm married, the rest of you can get your money. It's necessary."

"None of that money will help any of us if we have to watch you have a miserable marriage," Alexander said firmly. "There's something you're not telling me, Kat. I know it. So come on, out with it. You and me always shared the most secrets of anyone else here, didn't we? We were the closest of us all. Why should that change? Please, talk to me."

Katherine closed her eyes. She drew in a deep, fortifying breath, then moved from her dressing table to the bed, perching beside her brother. Alexander waited patiently for her to speak.

"I did intend to marry Lord Barwood when I first started to cultivate the acquaintance," she admitted. "He didn't seem as repulsive at first. It seemed to be the quickest and easiest solution. I'd already given up on the idea of finding love for myself. I thought… I thought if I could marry quickly, then the rest of you would have a little more time to choose somebody suitable. I thought we could get this whole wretched business over with as quickly as possible."

"But…?"

"But the more I got to know him, the more I realised I did not like him, not one bit. My situation hasn't changed, but... but I think I might be in love with someone else, Alexander."

Alexander's eyes widened. Whatever he'd been expecting to hear her say, it was not that.

"You... you're in love with someone else?"

Katherine swallowed hard, nodding. "I was ready to make a sacrifice, because I didn't know any better. The man I think I have feelings for – don't ask me who he is, I'm not ready to admit it aloud yet – is a good man. I think he'd made me happy, but I have no idea... no idea how he feels about me. I don't know if I can risk losing Lord Barwood for a man who... who may not think about me for a second more than he absolutely has to. Oh, I don't know what to *do*, Alex."

Alexander shuffled closer, wrapping an arm around her shoulder. Katherine sagged against him, resting her cheek on his chest. They sat like that together for a moment or two, and Katherine could have sworn that the years stripped themselves away, and they weren't adults with a tremendous amount of money hanging over their heads, but children with nothing to concern themselves with beyond dinner tonight and when they would get a chance to play outside.

"I can't marry him," Katherine said at last. "I can't marry Lord Barwood. I... I know that I should, but I don't think I can do it."

Alexander pressed a kiss to the top of her head. "I know, Kat. I know. Choose love for yourself – that's all I want. It's all William wants, too."

She shook her head. "William has so much to think about beyond me. It's not fair on him. None of this is fair on him."

"It's not fair on us, either."

The bell rang downstairs, signaling that breakfast was ready. Katherine sat up with a sigh, straightening the knot of hair at the nape of her neck.

"I assume that Lord Barwood is going to propose tonight," she said heavily. "I don't think I'll be able to avoid him. I think I should tell him the truth, before he does something foolish, like asking me to marry him in front of our guests."

"Oh, he wouldn't do anything so silly. The man hates to make himself look like a fool."

Katherine snorted. "Well, I made him look a fool at the party last night, so I daresay he's out for revenge."

"I'll stay with you all night. He won't be able to get you alone. Then, tomorrow, you can write a letter to him, explaining."

Katherine bit her lip. "A letter? That feels cowardly."

"There's nothing cowardly about rejecting a man like that," Alexander said firmly. "I'll talk to William, too. He'll understand, I know he will."

Katherine nodded, forcing a quick smile. "I hope I won't live to regret this."

***

The dinner was a fairly ordinary one – fine dishes, plenty of guests gathering around the table, plenty of chatter, and so on. The Duchess sat silently at one end of the table, speaking to no one, and William sat at the other end, equally quiet.

Katherine found herself between Lord Barwood and Alexander, who'd all but strong-armed another guest out of the way so that he could sit beside his sister. Even Henry was there tonight, although Katherine suspected that was because he was hungry, rather than from any sense of duty.

At a quiet moment at the table, she cleared her throat and leaned towards Lord Barwood, before nerves could get the better of her.

"I would like to speak to you about something later, Lord Barwood."

"Tell me now," he said, eyes scanning the table. Was he waiting for something?

"Not now," Katherine said firmly. "But later, perhaps. In private."

Lord Barwood drained his wine glass and gestured for the footman to refill it. "Just tell me now, why don't you?"

A flash of irritation went through her. "Later, Lord Barwood. I made that quite clear. I'm afraid it's not good news."

She wasn't sure what had made her say that. Lord Barwood shot a quick, thoughtful stare at her. For a moment, she thought he was going to push further, to insist on hearing what she wanted to say.

"Very well," he said at last, and she let out a sigh of relief. "As you like."

"Thank you."

More silence. Well, silence between the two of them, at least. Then, without warning, Lord Barwood rose to his feet. He tapped the edge of a fork against the rim of his glass, the clear tinkling sound slowly but surely cutting through the chatter, until everyone around him was silent.

Everybody was looking. Most of the guests were smiling inquisitively up at him, pleasantly confused, but Katherine saw strain and a flash of panic in William's face.

"Ladies and gentlemen," Lord Barwood said smoothly, smiling charmingly around. "I hope you're all enjoying your meal. I think the time has come to tell you now that there is an ulterior motive to your being here."

There was a chorus of *oohs* and *aahs*. A nasty feeling of foreboding began to curl in Katherine's gut. She felt sick.

"You will all know how highly I esteem Lady Katherine," here he paused to grin down at her, lifting his glass in a mock salute, "and how much I am esteemed in return."

People were nodding in agreement, smiling at him, smiling at Katherine.

No, she thought vaguely. *No, no, no.*

"And now the time has come to share with you all some exciting news," he continued.

Katherine felt as though she'd been turned to stone. She was aware that she should do *something* – what, exactly, she wasn't sure she knew – but her limbs seemed not to be responding to her. She could only stare up at Lord Barwood, offering no resistance when he leant down and picked up her hand, limp as a dead bird, and held it. She saw people's gazes flicker down to their entwined hands, and saw those people's faces soften and smile.

They think we're in love.

"I intend to make Lady Katherine my wife," Lord Barwood continued, "And she will then be my very own Lady Barwood. I have applied to her dear brother, William, for his consent which he has given," here he paused to lift his glass towards William, who was staring in shock, "and now that our engagement is official, the preparations for the wedding itself can begin."

On cue, the guests began to clap and cheer, offering congratulations. Lord Barwood accepted the congratulations for a moment or two, then lifted his glass into the air.

"Please join me in drinking to the health of my dearest betrothed, Lady Katherine. To your good health, my lady!"

There was a chorus of well-wishing, then everybody drained their glasses.

Well, not quite everybody. Alexander did not touch his glass. William was gripping his tightly, but he did not drink. Abruptly, Henry shoved his chair back from the table, so loudly and suddenly he made some of the other guests jump and stare in surprise. He glared at Lord Barwood, stared at his sister, then fixed a truly venomous glower on William. Then he turned on his heel and stamped out without another word, letting the door slam behind him.

"Perhaps we should have warned her brother ahead of time," Lord Barwood said sweetly, and was greeted by a few relieved chuckles.

Everybody was talking now, the words swinging around Katherine's head, making no sense at all. She glanced from face to face, seeing their smiles and meaningful nods, not returning any of them.

By tomorrow, the whole city will know that I'm engaged to Lord Barwood, she thought dumbly. *If I say that I am not engaged, that I never was, none of them will believe me. It'll count as me jilting him. He will be pitied and consoled, and I'll be an outcast. I'll never marry in time. Who'd want to marry a woman who has already jilted a man this Season? My life would be over.*

Oh, he's clever, indeed.

Katherine wondered briefly if Lord Barwood had intended to do this all along, or whether her comment about speaking to him later had made him realize that their relationship was coming to an end.

Either way, it was too late.

Katherine got mechanically to her feet, ignoring the comments and questions thrown her way. She was vaguely aware of one of her brothers calling her name, but really, it seemed to be coming from a hundred miles away.

"I am unwell," Katherine said to no one in particular, then turned on her heel and strode out of the dining room.

"My poor fiancé," she heard Lord Barwood saying behind her. "Too much excitement. Too many *novels*, I should think."

This was greeted by laughter. Nobody came after her.

Chapter Twenty-Two

The engagement was all over London. Of course, Timothy had heard it.

Lady Katherine Willoughby, engaged to Lord Geoffrey Barwood. Everybody had been expecting it, and nobody was surprised.

"They'll make a handsome couple," Amelia had remarked, although there was something in her voice which made Timothy think that perhaps not even she could get behind this marriage. "And everybody knew they had an *understanding*."

"I didn't think she liked him very much," Timothy had said.

They were taking tea in the family drawing room, with Lady Rustford presiding, when he'd heard the news. It was hard to keep still and react with composure.

"It's not about *liking* him," Constance scoffed. "It's a good match. And she's an odd one, everyone knows that. She'll get a lot of money, though."

Yes, and it'll go straight to him, Timothy thought sourly. Something heavy had landed in his stomach when he first heard the news. Something painful, something that wouldn't go away no matter how he twisted or shifted.

The engagement was official now. She wouldn't risk going back, because then she was almost certainly not to have an engagement for the rest of the Season, and Timothy knew that couldn't happen. He knew the truth.

He felt sick.

"I think I'd better go," he said, rising to his feet. He felt shaky, as if his knees might give out at any moment. "Thank you for the tea, Mother."

Lady Rustford nodded. She looked bored. Amelia, at least, looked anxious.

"You're leaving so soon, Timothy? Are you alright? Are you upset?"

"No," Timothy lied smoothly. "I'm not upset. Why would I be upset?"

She said nothing, and he left before he could think twice about it.

Timothy dashed off a quick note to William, asking him to meet in the club. They had a great deal to discuss.

He sat in their usual corner, nursing a brandy which was too soon in the day to drink, and tried to collect his thoughts.

What am I even going to say?

I'm love with your sister, Will. I'm well aware that she just agreed to marry another man, but could it be because she had no other options?

No, that sounded wrong. Besides, why was he assuming that he was a better choice than Lord Barwood?

Well, anyone who's ever met Lord Barwood would admit...

He paused, jerked out of his thoughts by a flurry of drunken laughter from across the club. One voice in particular was familiar.

Timothy got tentatively to his feet, craning his neck.

Oh, bother.

Sure enough, there was Lord Barwood, gathered with a clump of friends. They were clearly celebrating his engagement, and were roaring with tipsy laughter.

Wonderful. Timothy sat down with a thump, clenching his teeth against the sudden surge of anger welling up inside him.

"Sir, a message for you," a footman materialized at his elbow, handing over a neatly folded note with the Willoughby crest on it. Timothy guessed what it would say before he even opened it.

Sorry, Timothy. Can't meet today. Another time, though.

Your Friend, Will

So that was that, then. Timothy's chance to bare his heart to his friend was not going to work.

Probably for the best, he thought gloomily. *What were you going to say, anyway? What good would it do? Katherine's made her decision.*

He hunkered down as two laughing men staggered their way, leaning against the long, polished bar, snapping fingers at a distant footman. A quick glance over his shoulder told him that the men were Lord Barwood and a friend.

"She was having second thoughts, I could tell," Lord Barwood slurred. "So I went ahead with announcing the engagement. It's better in the long run, you know."

"Quite agree, old chap," the other man hiccupped. "Ladies often don't understand these things. Best not to let them be troubled with too many decisions, eh?"

"Amen, amen. I was thinking of asking the brother for an advance on her inheritance – heaven knows the bills are piling up for me – but I decided against it. They might think I'm only interested in her money."

"You *are* only interested in her money," the other man said, and they both chuckled.

"Well, she's rich enough, for a bluestocking, so I think I'll get myself a decent enough bargain," Lord Barwood remarked. "She's got so much money that I can pay off everything I owe *and* live a comfortable life. I could do much worse when it comes to heiresses – some of them tie everything up, so a husband is obliged to ask for an *allowance*, can you imagine?"

"Ridiculous," the man agreed. "A man's property is his property, after all, and that includes what belongs to his wife. Do you think Lady Katherine will kick up a fuss about you doing what you wish with her money?"

"I suspect she will, but none of that will matter. We'll be married, and by then, what I say will go. It's for the best. Her brothers will complain, but there won't be a thing they can do."

"Damned interfering fools."

"Don't swear in here, we'll be disbarred. Now, just be sure you keep your mouth shut about my debts, eh? I don't want the brothers to have an excuse to make her jilt me. She's not fond of me, but the engagement is official now, so if I don't make a mistake, she'll have to go ahead with it. I can almost smell the money. The sooner the better, I say."

"Agreed, my friend, agreed!"

More brandies arrived for Lord Barwood and his friend, and they drunk deeply.

Timothy got to his feet, leaving his own brandy. His stomach was churning too strongly for him to drink any of it, anyway. He strode right out of the club, directly past Lord Barwood and his friend. He heard his name called – he'd been recognized – but kept going, straight out into the road and into a stagecoach.

"Take me to the Dunleigh estate, please," he said shortly. "It's important. Please, drive quickly – I'll give you extra if we can get there as soon as possible."

The driver gave a grunt, pocketing the coin Timothy gave him.

"Right you are, sir. Right you are."

Chapter Twenty-Three

"There's nothing I can do," Katherine said, her voice much smaller than she'd intended. She'd practiced what she was going to say all the way to her friend's home, thinking it over and over. She would be brusque and straightforward – Elizabeth deserved the truth, and she deserved to hear it from Katherine.

She was too late. Elizabeth had heard it that morning – an acquaintance had dropped by right before breakfast, keen to share the news. And now here they were, talking in the parlour, sipping tea and pretending the world wasn't falling around their respective ears.

"You... you can't marry that man," Elizabeth said, voice wobbling. "You must see that, Kat. I can't stand him. He doesn't love you, I'd vouch for it, and you don't even *like* him. Once you're married, he'll have power over you. If he wants to stop you reading and studying, he can. If he wants to stop you seeing your family, from seeing *me*, he can do it. There's nothing anyone can do, not even William."

Katherine opened her mouth to argue, but nothing came out. There was nothing to say. Elizabeth was right – a man exercised absolute control over his wife. His sons would grow old enough to escape his authority, and a daughter could do the same, to an extent, or else get married and escape that way.

But a wife? A wife's subjugation was forever. That was why it was so important to marry the right man. So important to choose one's husband carefully. Very, very carefully.

Katherine felt sick. She'd felt sick continually since the party last night. After the announcement, the guests clearly felt that it was a surprise engagement party, and therefore felt entitled to stay as long as they liked, laughing and celebrating.

She wasn't sure how William and the others dealt with it. Henry had left the house, according to the butler, and Alexander went straight up to her room, trying to console her. It didn't do much good, and she soon asked him to leave. William stayed down with the guests. She supposed that he thought it was the right thing to do.

The Duchess came up to offer her congratulations shortly before bed, once everybody was gone. Katherine pretended to be asleep.

"You should tell him that you can't marry him," Elizabeth said.

"Things have already gone too far."

"No, they haven't. Right up until the day of your wedding, it's not too late."

Katherine scoffed. She bounced to her feet, pacing up and down the parlour. She wished she hadn't drunk the tea. It sloshed around in her empty stomach, making her feel sick. Over the past day, she'd spent her time nibbling on food and drinking, if only to fill the hole inside her.

"Let me paint you a picture, Elizabeth. I choose to break off the engagement to Lord Barwood. I can do that, and he nobly accepts. Very nobly, in fact. You can imagine how Society would react. Lord Barwood is handsome and superficially charming. People like him."

"People who don't know him."

"That's not the point. The point is the look of the thing. I would look like a monster."

"But you would be free," Elizabeth pointed out, setting down her teacup with a *clack*. "You'd be *free*, Kat. You can't marry him. You don't want to. I know you don't want to."

"That is true. But think of how long it would take for my reputation to recover. A woman jilting a fiancé is something that will interest the whole town. Everybody will have an opinion. They'll want to know why – why would I jilt such a handsome, charming man, especially when I'm such a bluestocking? They'll pity him, and they'll blame me. I'm sure he'll lean heavily into that. And then what about me? Nobody will touch me for the rest of the Season. Even next Season, people will be talking about me and my broken engagement. But, as you know, that will already be too late. Far too late. I have a limited amount of time, Elizabeth."

Elizabeth bit her lip, nodding her head. "You're right. You're right, Kat. I... I'm just so angry. You were strong-armed into a public betrothal, and now you're being marched towards the altar. I'm just so afraid for you, Katherine. So, so afraid."

"I'm afraid for me, too," Katherine responded, her voice small. Suddenly, she had no energy, and sank down onto the sofa again. Elizabeth moved over to sit beside her, reaching out to take her hand.

The two women sat there for a long moment, the grandfather clock ticking away the minutes.

Would it be the worst thing in the world, Katherine thought hazily, *if I just sat here forever? No deadline ticking away from me and my family, no fortune hanging over our heads. No Mother, slinking around, resenting us all, no William going slowly mad, no angry Henry, no drunk Alexander. No Lord Barwood dragging me towards the altar.*

She let out a tiny, stifled sob before she could stop herself.

"Oh, my love," Elizabeth murmured, pulling her into a tight hug. "Oh, Kat, you can't marry him."

"I must," Katherine sniffled. "It's just... well, if I wasn't in love with somebody else, perhaps I could bear it."

She'd expected surprise from Elizabeth, perhaps questions, maybe even demands. Instead, her friend simply tightened her arms around her.

"I know, sweetheart," Elizabeth murmured. "I know, I know. Please, at the very least, talk to William."

"William won't force me into anything else, but I know that we need my marriage. All of us need that. So, I'm going to go through with it. No point waiting to see if this... this other man might offer for me. I can't do that, Elizabeth. I can't do it to my family."

Elizabeth sighed. "I know you'll do what's right, Katherine. You always do what's right."

"Yes, I know," Katherine responded sourly. She had already decided that she would stay here another ten minutes, not a second more. It was time to go home and face her fate. No point in hiding. No point shrinking away. She was no coward, and she wasn't about to start acting like one now.

Chapter Twenty-Four

"Timothy!" William said, surprised, getting to his feet. "I... I wasn't expecting you. Did... did you not get the message I sent you? At the club? I would have liked to meet you, but I can't spare the time today..."

"I did get it," Timothy said, breathless. An overturned cart had brought traffic to a standstill, including the stagecoach, so Timothy had paid his fare and run the rest of the way, barging into the Willoughby house and into William's study.

William lifted an eyebrow. "Is... that is, can I help you with something?"

Timothy drew in a breath. He'd planned to spend the journey here rehearsing what he would say, but the frantic rush here had knocked it all out of his head. So, he just started speaking, letting the words spill out the way they did when he was writing.

"Lord Barwood is only marrying Katherine for her money," he said abruptly.

William's eyebrows climbed higher. "But he's a rich man."

"No. No, he's not. He has debts, lots of them. Investigate if you don't believe me. I overheard him talking about it in the club today."

William sucked in a breath. "You... truly? He said that about my sister?"

Timothy nodded. "I heard him. He doesn't care for her, and he's making no secret of it. He's celebrating right now, with his friends. He thinks he's got it made, and I... I can't let that happen."

William passed a shaking hand over his hair. "I can't believe it. I should have known, I should have..."

Timothy bit his lip. "How did this happen?"

William gestured bleakly for him to sit, and Timothy sat heavily in the seat opposite.

"I was scared for her," William said simply. "Scared for all of us. You know how much there is at stake. I let her pursue the courtship with Lord Barwood, because I thought that was her only option. Stupid, really. I should have been protecting her, doing my duty, instead of..."

"This isn't your fault," Timothy said quietly.

"Oh, you're sure? Let me tell you this. The man asked for my consent, and I gave it, and told him to talk to her first. The next thing I knew, he was standing up at the dining room table, announcing their engagement. I had no idea. Neither did Katherine, for that matter. He'd never spoken to her about it. I should have intervened then and there, should have thrown him out of our home and set the record straight. Instead, I just sat there and let him say what he wanted. I'm disgusted at myself, Timothy. Do you still feel so sympathetic towards me?"

Timothy bit his lip. "You're still not to blame. I... I have some things to tell you, Will."

"Go on."

Timothy drew in a deep breath, steadying himself.

"I'm L. Sterling, William."

There was a long pause.

"The... the novelist?" William stammered. "Are you serious?"

"I'm deadly serious, Will. You know I always wanted to write. I never thought I could write, but I can. I wrote my first novels, and they did so well, then I wrote more and more, and now I'm... now I'm L. Sterling."

William let out a long, slow breath. "Well. I'd say that I was surprised, but frankly, I don't think I am. I could always see you as a writer. If you don't mind me asking, why are you telling me now?"

"Because I'm tired of hiding. Tired of pretending that I'm something I'm not. And I want you to know that while I'm not rich, I can take care of myself. I don't take a penny of my father's money."

William leaned forward, patting Timothy's hand where it rested on the table.

"I know. You're a good man, Tim. Everybody knows that."

Timothy closed his eyes. "I'm trying to tell you that I'm in love with Katherine."

There was a pregnant pause.

"Y...you?" William managed. "You're in love with Katherine? Is this a favour, to get her away from Lord Barwood? Because if so..."

"No," Timothy said firmly. "No, it's not that. I couldn't tell you when I started falling in love with Katherine, but I know that it has happened. I can't think of anyone but her. I'm not asking your permission to court her, William. I'm not asking your permission to marry her. I know Katherine, and I know you, and I know that there's only one person who I need to speak to about this. I just... I just wanted to tell you, because you're my friend. That, and I'm tired of hiding. Tired of pretending. I feel like a coward, and I'm going to put all of that behind me."

He drew in a deep breath after this speech. It felt like a real weight off his shoulders. Who would have known that it was such a *relief*?

William blinked, eyes wide.

"Well, that is... that is unexpected. You want to talk to Katherine right now?"

"If you don't mind, yes."

William shook his head slowly. "Well, as you said, you don't need my permission. I don't think I'll give it – Katherine's already annoyed enough at me giving my permission to Lord Barwood, so I think it's best if you handle this yourself. But at the moment, she's not here – she's gone to see her friend, Elizabeth."

On cue, the sound of carriage wheels on gravel sounded up the drive. Both men rose slowly to their feet, moving across to the window.

Timothy watched the carriage roll to a halt in front of the house, and saw Katherine delicately pick her way down. She didn't immediately go inside. Instead, she drew in a few deep breaths, tilting back her head, letting the sun play over her face. She reached up, taking off her bonnet, letting it dangle by her side.

Timothy was transfixed.

At last, Katherine opened her eyes, glancing at the house. She looked exhausted.

Seeming to decide something, she let her bonnet flutter to the ground, turned on her heel, and walked away into the gardens, never once looking back.

Timothy glanced over at William, raising his eyebrows.

"Go," William said at once. "Go on, Timothy. Go and see her. I'll... I'll wait in here. You can come in and have tea afterwards, if you like. Or... or don't."

"Thank you." Timothy turned to go, but paused when William called his name.

"Congratulations on the novels," William said, blushing. "They're excellent."

Chapter Twenty-Five

Katherine collapsed on the first stone bench she found, letting the air gust out of her lungs in one long sigh.

So this is it, then, she thought miserably. *My life begins and ends here. I marry a man who doesn't care about me, all because of my selfish father's will. And now there's no way out of it.*

Wonderful.

She tilted back her head, letting the sun play over her face, and closed her eyes.

How will I bear it?

She heard crunching footsteps over the gravel but didn't immediately turn around. William would likely have seen her coming from his study window and might have sent somebody out to fetch her. Or perhaps he would even have come himself.

"You dropped this."

She flinched at Timothy's voice, eyes flying open. He was holding out her bonnet, smiling wryly down at her.

"Oh. Thank you," Katherine managed, taking the bonnet from him. She rose nervously to her feet. "I… I suppose that you've heard the news."

"That you're marrying Lord Barwood? Yes, I heard. And yes, I am here to convince you not to go ahead with it."

Katherine shook her head. "I have to, you know that. You know the situation we're in – I know that William told you – and the fact is that I *must* marry. It's as simple as that."

Timothy seemed to waver, lips moving as if sounding through words. She found herself waiting, breathless, for him to speak.

It was pleasant, being around a man who weighed his words so carefully.

A man who sent her heart fluttering the way Timothy did. A pang sounded through Katherine's chest.

How will I bear it when I'm married to another man?

"I... I have a confession to make," he said slowly. "I didn't come straight here to confront you about this. I went home first. Made the stagecoach wait."

Katherine lifted an eyebrow. "I... see. Why should I care about that? No offence."

"None taken. I went home to pick up this."

He reached into his jacket and took out a thick sheaf of papers. It took Katherine a moment to realize that she was looking at a manuscript.

"It's not finished, but read the front page," he said quietly, handing it to her. The front page was a blank sheet, with just a few typed words in the centre.

Rosalie's Redemption (Rosalie's Trials, Vol III)
Written by Mr. Timothy Rutherford (publishing name L. Sterling)

Katherine stared at the words until her vision swam.

"I... I... I don't understand," she gasped. "What is this?"

"It's the final book of the *Rosalie* instalments," Timothy said, eyes fixed on her. "I wrote the *Rosalie* books. I wrote all of them. I'm L. Sterling, Katherine."

All of a sudden, everything he had said and done came crashing back on, so painfully obvious that Katherine wasn't sure whether she wanted to laugh, cry, or manage both at the same time.

"You're L. Sterling," she managed at last, hand fluttering up to her mouth.

"I should have told you, but I had no idea you liked my novels that much, and then it just seemed... just seemed like I would be courting attention."

"Your books are remarkable," she admitted. "When I read them, I feel... I feel whole again."

He shrugged lightly. "When I write them, I feel whole. I only now told William, for what it's worth. I've kept this secret from everybody I know. I intend to keep it secret, too. I don't want fame, I just want to write in peace. But you… I want you to know."

She swallowed hard, nodding. "I… I understand."

He stepped forward, hand coming out to rest on her forearm. The warmth of his fingers seemed to burn, in a good way.

"Katherine, don't marry him," he said softly. "Please. I beg you, don't marry him. He only wants you for your money, I overheard him saying it in the club."

Katherine shook her head. "That doesn't surprise me. But I must marry someone, Timothy. You know that."

"I do know that." He drew in a deep breath. "Katherine, marry me."

Her head shot up. "What? Timothy, I can't let you do that. I can't let you… let you sacrifice yourself for me."

Timothy clenched his jaw. "I love you, Katherine."

The words hung in the air, and she wasn't entirely sure that she hadn't imagined them.

"What did you say?" Katherine breathed.

Timothy took another step closer, so that there was only half a breath between them. His hand was still on her forearm, and Katherine found that her other arm had slid up to rest on his shoulder. It might be somewhat dramatic, but she felt as if she tore her gaze away from his now, she would die.

"I am not offering to marry you because of the will," Timothy said firmly. "I don't care about that. I love you, Katherine, and I have loved you for a long time."

"Why… why did you never say anything?"

"Because I was afraid. Afraid that I would lose you, *and* William, afraid of rejection, I suppose. Growing up with my parents, I had to face a great deal of rejection, and none of it was pleasant. I suppose I thought that putting my head in the sand and pretending that what I felt was just friendship was the simplest way to manage what I felt. I was wrong. I know you're too honest with yourself and too kind to marry me if you don't feel anything for me, so don't feel as though…"

"Yes," Katherine gasped, before her head even caught up with her tongue. "Yes, Timothy, I will marry you – if you really mean it, that is."

He gave a short, breathless laugh. "Of course I mean it. I don't think I've ever meant anything more in my life. I... I love you, Katherine."

"I love you too, Timothy. I think perhaps I loved you even before I knew you wrote the best novels I've ever read in my life."

Then Timothy's arms were around her, and Katherine pulled him close, arms looped around his neck, and they were kissing, even though it was entirely improper for them to be kissing out here, old friends or not.

She was, after all, *engaged to another man*, although Katherine was not thinking about Lord Barwood at that exact moment, and had the strangest, creeping feeling that she was never going to think about him ever again.

Epilogue

One Month Later

Katherine eyed the letter nervously, as if she were afraid, it might bite her.

"And you're sure Father intended for me to open this letter on my wedding day?" she enquired nervously.

Mr Thompson shifted his position. It was clear he did not feel comfortable being in the house during the chaos of Katherine's wedding, not when there was so much legal paperwork to straighten up. After all, after today, Katherine was going to be a remarkably wealthy woman. Then, only the boys needed to find themselves spouses, and the Willoughby fortune would be complete again.

"Quite sure," Mr Thompson said firmly. "The late Duke made it clear that each one of his children is to receive a handwritten letter, prepared by himself ahead of time, on the day of their wedding. This is yours. You have the pleasure of being the first to read your letter."

"Hardly a choice, was it?" Katherine remarked sourly. "I was forced to marry."

Mr Thompson inclined his head. "I was under the impression that yours and Mr Rutherford's marriage is to be a love-match."

She flushed. "Yes, it is. I shouldn't be ungrateful, I suppose. Without Father's... *interfering*, I should never have found Timothy. I would never have realised how I felt for him."

"Indeed," said Mr Thompson, looking uncomfortable. "I shall leave you to read."

He got up, leaving Katherine alone in her bedroom, sitting in her wedding finery. She eyed the crisp white envelope with distaste. Would it be the worst thing in the world to toss it into the fire and have done with it?

Probably.

Before she could give herself a chance to change her mind, Katherine snatched up the envelope, tore it open, and began to read. Her father's spiky scrawl of handwriting was as familiar as ever.

To My Daughter.

You and I were never close, Katherine. You were not what I wanted in a daughter, and I daresay I was not what you wanted in a father. No doubt you resent me for the will I left behind, and the terms imposed upon you. I will not apologise – I felt that those terms were necessary, and I still do.

I believe that marriage is important in every person's life. I believe that we were, as humans, created in pairs, and it is our life's goal to find our other half. Say what you will about your mother and me, but I know that she loves me greatly, and I have always done my best to be a worthy husband to her. Your mother was a duchess in her prime, and a noble lady. I meant to superintend the marriages of each of my children, but lately, my thoughts turn to death. My own father died young, and I am aware that some accident may befall me. So, I have made preparations to compel each of you to marry in order to earn your inheritance.

But you, Katherine, are stubborn. I could imagine you simply refusing to marry, and therefore letting your part of the Willoughby fortune slip away. That is why the will stipulates that you must marry first, before any of your brothers may claim their inheritance.

No doubt you resent me for this and think it harsh. Perhaps you are right. I am not a good man, and I have made a great many mistakes in my life.

My four children, however, do not number among my mistakes.

Think kindly of me, Katherine. Know that in my own way, I did love you.

Oh, before I go, let me say who I would have chosen for you, should I have had the chance to manage your marriage.

Money is not a problem for us, so I would have chosen a man with other qualities. In point of fact, I always liked Lord Rustford's son. Not the oldest boy, but the one who was always William's friend. I cannot recall his name now, but I think he would have made you happy.

*Regards,
Your Father,
The Duke of Dunleigh*

Katherine swallowed down a heavy lump in her throat, carefully folding up the letter.

It didn't undo what their father had put them through, of course. He was *not* a good father, there was no denying that, but... well, it was something.

He would have picked Timothy for me, she thought, a single tear spilling down her cheek. *How strange.*

Then the sounds rushed in from outside, and Katherine remembered that this was her wedding day, and she needed to get to the church as soon as possible. Wiping away the stray tear, she tweaked her curls into place and gave herself one last, appraising look in the mirror. On cue, somebody banged on the door. Elizabeth, no doubt, the only person in the house with her eye on the clock.

"Kat! We need to go!"

"I'm ready!"

***

William was poised to escort his sister down the aisle, his heart filled with joy for her impending nuptials. And yet, a strange encounter at the masquerade ball lingered in his thoughts, distracting him from the celebratory occasion. The lady with the silver locket had captivated his attention, and now he clutched the locket in his hand, longing for answers to the mystery that had ensnared him.

The church was full. Alexander and Henry, dressed in their Sunday best, were waiting in their pews, while William escorted Katherine down the aisle. He appeared preoccupied, as though something weighed heavily on his mind, Katherine thought. She also observed another peculiar detail; he held her with one hand while his other was clenched into a fist, as though grasping onto something tightly. That seemed strange and she noted to ask him after the wedding. A few people were conspicuous by their absences – Lord Barwood, for example, was *not* there, because he was in debtor's prison – but everybody Katherine cared about was there.

I'm getting married, she thought dizzily. *I'm getting married to the love of my life.*

The Duchess smiled weakly at her, and Katherine made herself smile back. Her relationship with her mother would take a great deal of fixing up, but Katherine was determined to make the effort if her mother was.

You never knew.

They reached the top of the aisle, and William gave her a quick peck on the cheek.

"You look beautiful, sister," he murmured.

"You'll all be following me soon, I hope," she remarked, and earned herself an eye roll.

And then it was just Katherine and Timothy, standing side by side in their wedding finery, and the rest of the world just melted away.

"Hello," Timothy whispered.

Katherine smiled. "Good morning."

"I have some news."

The priest began to drone on, but neither of them were listening.

"Oh?"

Timothy smiled nervously. "The book... the last *Rosalie* book that is... I finished it. It's done. I completed it last night, and I'm going to send off the copy to the publisher after our wedding."

Katherine grinned. "Oh, that's excellent news. I do have one stipulation, as you brand-new wife and therefore somebody very important in your life."

"Oh, yes? Do tell?"

She dropped a wink, entirely inappropriate for a wedding, even her own.

"I want to read it first."

The End

Printed by Amazon Italia Logistica S.r.l.
Torrazza Piemonte (TO), Italy